The Cloud People

KENARD TUZENEU

ISBN 979-8-88616-508-1 (paperback)
ISBN 979-8-88616-509-8 (digital)

Christian Faith Publishing
832 Park Avenue
Meadville, PA 16335
www.christianfaithpublishing.com

Printed in the United States of America

Contents

Summer Vacation—At Last

I had barely slept in days. I was so distracted during those last few weeks of school that I was always getting in trouble with my teacher. Even Lucas, one of my best friends, was annoyed with me and didn't want to hang out on the playground. I know I was acting weird, but all I could think about was what I imagined would be the best summer ever. In just a few days, I would be leaving for a week to stay with my grandparents in Indiana. My family visited them every summer for as long as I can remember, but this time was different. This time I was going by myself! I was excited and nervous at the same time. I couldn't wait to see my grandparents, but I have to admit, the thought of flying without my family was a little scary.

Dad was going away on business at the same time, and I knew Mom would be busy driving my little sister to all her games. I guess it was a good thing that I was leaving town! That morning, the one thing I did not want to forget was my new camera. I kept checking my luggage to make sure it was packed. For sure, I was going to be taking *a lot* of pictures. I had begged my parents for that camera for at least a year, and they finally came through for my birthday. It was awesome—a 35-millimeter digital power shot, 16.1 megapixel, with a 16-gig memory card, and really cool zoom lens. It was even water and dirt proof. Not only was I going to be taking a mess of pictures, I was planning on making a photo journal of the trip—for me, but I also thought Mom and Dad and, yes, even little Sis, would like to see them.

Dad had already said goodbye that morning. I would really miss him. He was great to hang out with, especially over the summer, but I really wished he could have at least come to the airport. If only Dad was around, at least he would have been able to calm her down.

Mom was *so* nervous she was driving me crazy. "Are you sure you have everything? Are you sure you're going to be okay by yourself? If you have any questions, just ask someone in uniform…" "Yes, Mom. Okay, Mom. Don't worry. I'll be fine." She sometimes forgets how grown up I am. She still liked to say, "Billy, you'll always be my baby." That embarrassed me to no end. Oh well, at least it is nice to know she cares.

Her list of questions almost made me forget my camera. It's a good thing I checked one last time because I had actually left it in my room. I ran back inside, grabbed it off my bed, and dashed back downstairs. My heart was pounding, not so much from running but from the anticipation. I was finally leaving on my great journey. There was no way I could have known that it would turn out to be an even greater adventure than I imagined.

As we pulled away from the house, my imagination wandered off to my grandparents' house. They have the neatest porch with the best swing. I was already seeing myself there, enjoying a cool summer breeze. I was distracted from my daydreaming by the big puffs of clouds I saw in the sky as I looked out the window of the car. I loved looking at clouds. These though were especially big. They looked as if someone had hung large balls of cotton in the sky. I was wrapped up in looking for different images in the clouds when my sister tapped me on the shoulder.

"Hey, Billy. Let's play our game!"

Every time we were in the car together, we challenged each other to see who could name the most trees and plants. We took turns. At first, it was easy, but the longer we drove, the harder it became. I usually tried to get one past her by making up some names. She always caught me though. The airport wasn't that far from home, so we didn't have much time to play. We were in the middle of a furious argument over one of my made-up tree names when we arrived.

"Saved by the airport!" she said, for she wasn't about to give up her challenge to my fake name.

As I was getting more excited, poor Mom was getting all nervous again. I jumped out of the car and ran back to the trunk. Just as I grabbed my bag, Mom's cell phone rang. It was Dad! Mom only held it for a second and then handed it to me.

"He wants to say goodbye."

I'm not sure which made me happier—that he called, or that he would calm Mom down.

"Really sorry I couldn't come. Well, son, have a great time. I'll be in touch while you're out there. Tell Grandma and Grandpa we all said hello."

After finishing, I gave the phone back to Mom. When Dad called us, she was always the last to talk. Unlike some of my friends' parents, Mom and Dad really loved each other. I heard her say, "I'm fine, a little nervous, but I'll be okay—and so will Billy. See you soon. Love you."

As we walked into the airport, we were met by a pretty lady. She walked over to Mom and extended her hand. "My name is Liz. I'm the guardian for your son. We'll take good care of him."

With that, it was finally time. Sis couldn't resist one last dig. "Have a good time, and oh, by the way, you know I won the naming game!"

I wasn't about to let that go, trip or no trip, but Mom intervened. "Okay. That's enough. It's time to go. Let's call it a tie." With that, she gave me a big hug and a smile. "Be safe, now and don't do anything foolish. Behave with Grandma and Grandpa. Call as soon as you get there."

"Don't worry, Mom. I'll be fine."

As Liz and I walked to the check-in counter, I turned and gave Mom and Sis one last wave. Just then, I realized that I forgot my camera! I was sure that I had grabbed it and put it around my neck. It wasn't there. I couldn't believe it. Not my camera! I tried so hard to remember it, and now it was too late. Mom had already left. I was so mad at myself. At the time, I was just upset that I forgot my cool new camera. Little did I know how much I would wish I had remembered it.

The Flight

At first, I was a little annoyed that I had to have a guardian to take me to the plane. As it turned out, with Liz guiding me, we breezed through all the security in no time. Wow. I guess having her was worth it, besides keeping Mom calm! When we got to the gate, I was first in line to get on the plane—even better. Liz handed me over to the person at the counter who walked me to my seat. I was getting used to all this attention. I felt like a celebrity.

When I got to my seat, I was thrilled to be next to the window. Each time we went to see my grandparents, I was fortunate enough to be by the window. I loved looking outside. It was always so cool. As soon as I sat down, I buckled my seatbelt to get that out of the way. I didn't want to listen to that boring preflight speech. I knew the routine. Besides, I just wanted to look outside. I was always fascinated with all the activity around the plane—people loading the luggage (I checked to see if I could see mine), loading the food, and other people moving around doing whatever they do. There was a lot to see. Before I knew it, it was time for takeoff. I sat back, ready for my vacation.

Just before the plane started to move, I again looked out at the sky. I could still see those big fluffy clouds floating across the sky. They had so many shapes and designs. For a brief moment, I remembered studying all about clouds in school. I much preferred seeing castles and animals than remembering what they were made of or what they were called. I guess that's one reason I was always getting in trouble for not paying attention!

My mind was pulled back from flashing back to school as I heard the roar of the engines. As we picked up speed, I imagined what it would be like if I could take off like the plane. It would be so neat to fly. In an instant, we were up in the air and making a big turn to get on course. As we did, I could see the clouds right out my window. It looked as if I could actually reach out and touch them. What a sight! I imagined floating among the clouds, and before I knew it, I was fast asleep. That had never happened during any of my other trips. I guess all the excitement and running around before I left caught up with me. That little nap made the flight seem like an instant, for no sooner had I closed my eyes, I heard the announcement to get ready for landing. We would be on the ground in twenty minutes!

I was so thrilled that I would soon see my grandparents. I could already see myself racing down the runway to meet them. It's funny how those last few minutes of the flight always take so long. Oh well, we were almost on the ground. I already had my seat in the "upright and locked position." That's when I saw it. After adjusting my seat, I happened to look out my window. There it was!

Again, there were a bunch of big fluffy clouds all around the plane. I think this time there were almost twice as many as I saw when I left. As I glanced through the clouds imagining all kinds of things, to my surprise, suddenly, right in the middle, I saw what looked like a face! This wasn't just another shape in the clouds that I was imagining. It was an actual face! It looked like a person lying on top of the clouds made out of cotton. The eyes were closed, as if it was sleeping. Then I thought, as real as it looked, it had to be my imagination. That would have made sense, except for what I saw next. The eyes on the face opened! Not only did they open, but they looked directly at me. I was looking straight into his eyes, and he was looking right back at me. It wasn't my imagination. I know, whatever it was, looked at me. Suddenly, the expression on the cloud face changed, and it appeared as if whatever, or whoever it was, had a look of panic. It acted as if he just got caught. It seemed to me that it was thinking it shouldn't have been seen. Then in a flash, it was gone.

I leaned closer to the window to search the clouds to try to find whatever that was I just saw. As hard as I looked, I couldn't find it. It reminded me of the many times I saw deer in my backyard at home. They would stare at me, but as soon as I started to walk toward them, they would jump into the woods. Just like disappearing deer, the face was gone—but I knew I saw it.

I completely forgot about landing and seeing my grandparents and, well, pretty much everything. Without thinking, I took off my seat belt so I could lift myself up to look out the window. I continued to search through the clouds even though I wasn't having any success. What was it? I know I didn't imagine it! Were there more? How could it be?

Just then I heard a stern voice right next to me. "Please sit down and buckle your seat belt. We are about to land!"

I turned around and saw the stewardess staring right at me. Oops! I sat down and buckled in, but as soon as she left, I turned to look back out the window, with my seatbelt buckled! No luck! I didn't see anything. Whatever I saw, it was gone.

I could already hear my parents saying to me, "Billy, you and your imagination! Forget about it. You know that's impossible." Still, I know what I saw. This was different. Surely someone else saw it. I didn't care what anybody thought. I had to find another witness.

As everyone got their stuff and prepared to leave the plane, I started asking other passengers the same question, "Excuse me. Did you see anything unusual outside the plane when we were landing?"

A few just smiled at me, most ignored me, and then there were those that were plain annoyed with me. One older woman snapped back at me, "Look, young man. I don't have time for your silly games. Besides, I don't know what kind of parents would let a boy like you fly by himself."

I wanted to say something, but I was always taught to be polite, so I settled for saying, "Never mind," but then mumbled under my breath, "Grouch!"

A younger woman standing behind me saw that whole exchange. She gave me a gentle pat on the shoulder and whispered, "Don't let her bother you. It's okay. She must just be in a hurry. Oh, and by the way. I'm sorry, I didn't see anything unusual." She gave me a nice smile, which made me feel better, but I was so bummed out that I couldn't find anybody who saw that face. No other witnesses. Darn!

Grandparents

As I walked off the plane, I was met by another lady from the airline who introduced herself.

"I'm Becky, your guardian here in the airport. I'm going to take you to your grandparents. Just follow me. They are so excited to see you. They can't wait!"

For the moment, I forgot about the clouds and focused on meeting my grandparents and starting my vacation. I loved my grandparents and was now about to see them. At school, some of my friends made fun of me for talking about them so much. I didn't care. They were great people. As Becky led me down the ramp, I looked up, and there they were! I had arrived in Indiana.

"We have been looking forward to this for weeks! It's great that you are finally here." Grandma gave me one of her best hugs. My grandfather grabbed my hand and gave me his firm handshake. Then he pulled me up into his arms and gave me a big hug. It was a good feeling.

"Me too. I couldn't wait either." I looked at Grandma. "By the way, what's for dinner?"

Grandma was a great cook, and I have to admit that one of things that made these vacations so terrific was the food, not that Mom was a bad cook!

"Guess," Grandma said with delight.

She loved to cook but mostly for company. It gave her great joy to have her family and friends enjoy a good meal. Without hesitation, I mentioned my favorite, really hoping that I was right. "Chicken pot pie?"

Grandma beamed from ear to ear. She knew it was my favorite. "You're right, Billy. Chicken pot pie it is."

"All right! I knew it!"

Now that I knew what we were having for dinner, I turned my attention to Grandpa. He gave me another big hug.

"Billy, you look great. Wow, you're getting bigger and stronger. I can't wait to have you help with some chores on the farm," he said with a big grin.

Actually, he no longer had a farm. He told us many stories from his days growing up on that farm and working it for many years. It had been closed from even before I was born, but he still loved to tease about working his farm. Part of me wished it was still a farm, even though a lot of my friends thought that was lame. There was just such a cool feeling when I was there. Maybe it was a nice break from my suburban life, but I looked forward to my time with him in the country.

"I can't wait either, Grandpa. Put me to work!"

All around me, I could see families greeting one another. It was noisy, but it was a neat sight. It was almost as if the plane had been filled only with people travelling to be with family. But the joy of the moment was interrupted when Grandpa asked his usual question, "How was your flight?"

He asked it every time I flew, and I knew it was coming. It was just that this time, it struck me different. All of a sudden, I found myself back on the plane and seeing that face in the cloud, a face that only I had seen. I wanted so badly to tell Grandpa, but I knew better. I didn't dare, so I managed a standard answer.

"Oh, Grandpa, it was great. Nothing unusual. Well, there was this grumpy woman but, oh well, never mind that. Yea, it was a good flight."

I smiled to myself as I recalled the satisfaction of mumbling to her, "Grouch!" Fortunately, they accepted my answer without comment. By then, we had grabbed my luggage, and we were walking to their car. At last, my vacation was officially beginning. We were heading for the "farm" and chicken pot pie!

As soon as we pulled into the "farm," my heart started racing. I loved this place! I immediately recognized every tree, bush, and bit of grass. It was as if I had never left. When Grandpa stopped the car, I jumped outside and ran to my favorite tree. Just as I began to climb, Grandma called me back.

"Billy, don't forget your suitcase." The tone in her voice was kind but firm. They took great care of me during my visits, but I was expected to pull my weight. That began with bringing in my own stuff.

Obediently, I jumped down and ran back to the car. I would have plenty of time to finish climbing that great old tree. I grabbed my suitcase and small backpack out of the trunk. I stopped for just a moment to take it all in. It was a perfect day, and I was finally here. Yup, I loved this place!

"Billy, when you finish putting your stuff in your room, get washed up. We're going have company for dinner."

I wondered who it could be, but I had pretty good idea. Suppertime at my grandparents' house was always special. I couldn't wait—besides, I realized how hungry I was!

I threw my stuff on the bed and went over to the window to look out at the yard. The sky was mostly sunny, but there were some clouds floating around. The sight of the clouds took my thoughts away from dinner. I began searching the sky through my window, again wondering to myself if I really saw what I think I did. I kind of hoped that I might see something, any sign of my mystery sighting, but it was just an ordinary bunch of clouds—interesting and all but no faces! Oh well, at least I'm having pot pie for dinner. I quickly washed up and came downstairs.

"So, Grandma, who's coming for dinner?"

"Well, Uncle Frank is coming. He has vacation time, so he'll be spending the week with us."

Uncle Frank was my grandmother's brother's oldest son. I explained that to my friends a zillion times, but they never got it. "He's my mother's cousin, and I call him uncle." His father had died when he was young, so he looked up to Grandpa as his dad. They had a great relationship, and I really liked him too, even though he was a little different.

"I invited the Bensons, but the twins are sick."

The Bensons were an interesting family. Mr. Benson's parents were one of only a few African American families in the area. They had died before I even met Mr. Benson. He was their only son, and he served in the army, like my grandfather. He was stationed in Germany, and that's where he met his wife. They moved back to Indiana, so like my grandfather, he was living in the house in which he grew up. The Benson's and my grandparents had always been great friends. They didn't live too far away, and I saw them every time I visited. The little boys were funny, but Megan was my best friend. Even from a distance, we grew up together. We always kept in touch. I really hoped she was coming.

"What about Megan? Is she coming?"

"Don't worry," Grandma said. "Her dad is bringing her."

"Great! Oh, I mean I'm sorry the twins are sick, but I'm glad Megan is coming. I can't wait to see her."

"I know. I know," Grandma said.

Well, this was a fantastic way to start my vacation—Megan, my best friend, and my wacky but cool Uncle Frank and my favorite dinner.

Dinner

As I was in the middle of helping Grandma finish setting the table, there was a knock at the door. I knew who it was.

"Hey. The war hero is here!" announced Grandpa.

Sure enough, in walked Uncle Frank. He had been a helicopter pilot during Vietnam. He always had stories to tell. It wasn't until recently I realized that some of them were either made up or enhanced when he had an audience. Actually, I don't think he liked to talk about the real stories of the war. If someone asked a serious question, he would get this strange look in his eyes and give a short answer or change the subject.

"Uncle Frank, look who's here!" I shouted as I held my hands out to my side in dramatic fashion.

"Hey, buddy! How are you? You look great. Are you shrinking?" Uncle Frank loved to tease, and he knew I was sensitive about being short. Somehow when he busted me though, I didn't mind. I was ready for him.

"Yea, that happened just after I was abducted by the aliens last winter. I must have lost at least four inches."

Uncle Frank didn't say anything but shot me a look and a thumbs-up as if to say, "Good one!" But he wasn't quite done. "Well, I wonder if it was the same ones that got me ten years ago?"

I realized that Uncle Frank would always get in the last word. "Okay. You win! Hey, Uncle Frank, when did you grow that beard?"

I suddenly noticed that he had a big bushy beard that gave him a bit of a wild appearance, but his kind eyes seemed to offset the fierceness.

"This? Gosh, I guess I've had it for about a year. That's right. I haven't seen you for a while. Well, it started during one of my trips when I forgot my razor, then it just kept growing. Now I'm used to it. So what do you think?"

"Looks good, Uncle Frank. Besides, it makes up for what you're missing up top!"

Of course, Uncle Frank wouldn't stop there, but I was literally saved by the bell—well, another knock at the door! Mr. Benson was at the door, and with him, Megan.

It was great to see them, and within minutes, we were all caught up on the latest family happenings. I was mostly excited to see Megan though. Not only was she my age, but she was great to hang out with. I sure wished she lived next door back home.

Mr. Benson excused himself, "Well, I have to get back home. Good to see you, Billy. Goodbye all. Megan, see you later. Have a good time."

As soon as he walked out the door, I turned to her. "Hey, Megan, I bet I can still beat you climbing up the tree!"

"That's what you think." And before I knew it, she was on her way out the porch door. I was right behind her when Grandma stopped the race, which was probably fortunate because Megan had a good head start!

"Nobody's climbing any trees. Dinner is almost ready. Here's something to drink and munch on while I finish getting everything ready."

We both came back in, and Megan bumped into me and whispered, "I had you, and you know it!"

I wanted to reply, but I quickly turned my attention to some iced tea and snacks. I hadn't had anything to eat since I left my house earlier that day. Everyone continued to chat, and I dove into the goodies and gulped my drink.

I couldn't believe that I was finally here. I had been waiting for this for so long, and now here I am at my grandparents' house, with Megan and Uncle Frank. As everyone was talking, very innocently but without warning, just like Grandpa had done, Megan asked *the* question. It was to be expected, but with an audience, it really shook me. "It's great to have you here, Billy. So *how was your flight?*"

I was focused on being here and wasn't thinking about clouds. Her question brought it all back. I didn't know what to say. I wanted to avoid the question, but something inside of me had to tell her. Megan was my best friend, and I knew I could trust her. Without giving it any more thought, and before I answered, I called out, "Grandma, when will dinner be ready? Do I have a few minutes?"

"You have *ten* minutes," she said.

"Okay. Can Megan and I go out on the porch? We're not going to race. I just want to…" I couldn't think of what to say, but I had to talk to her before I burst. "I just want to show her something."

"Okay, Billy, but make it quick. Dinner is almost ready," Grandma said.

I knew I only had a few moments, so I grabbed Megan's hand and said, "Come on. Let's go. I just want to show you something outside."

Grandpa looked up and just smiled, but Uncle Frank shot me a look that told he was suspicious, but he didn't say anything. Well, it didn't matter. We were out the door. By her expression, I could tell Megan knew something was up.

When we got outside, Megan immediately pulled her hand away and blurted out, "Okay, Billy. What's going on? Something's on your mind."

I took a quick look back inside to make sure no one was listening. I pushed Megan to the edge of the porch. I sat down and, pulling her arm, said, "Here. Sit next to me. I just have to tell you something." By now it was obvious that she knew something was bothering me.

Well, I had her attention, but now I couldn't decide how to begin. Finally, I just blurted it out. "Megan, you're not going to believe this, but I saw something when I was on the plane. I still can't believe it myself, but I know what I saw."

Words were just flying out of my mouth, and Megan just stared back at me. I thought I was making sense, but from the look on her face, I could tell she wasn't getting it.

"Billy, slow down. What are you talking about? So far, all I've got is that you saw something on the plane. Relax. It's no big deal. Just tell me."

I took a deep breath and tried to relax. I was just so afraid that she would think that I was crazy or something. So far, I think she imagined that I was talking about something *inside* the plane. What would she think when I told her the truth? Just at that moment, I heard Grandma calling, "Megan. Billy. Come on in. Dinner is ready!"

At first, I was relieved, but I also knew that I would burst if I didn't tell her. I had to tell *someone*, and I think Megan was the best choice to hear it first. With literally no time to think and knowing that dinner was waiting, I finally decided to tell her, plainly and calmly, "When I was on the plane, I looked out the window, and I saw a person in the clouds." Immediately realizing that she could misunderstand, I repeated it with even greater firmness: "No, I didn't see somebody floating in the clouds. I didn't see clouds in the form of a person. I saw a *person*, a real person. I don't know, a cloud person. This face, with eyes and everything, looked right at me. It looked surprised, and then it disappeared in the clouds."

There was a moment of silence as Megan tried to absorb what I just told her. I didn't expect what happened next. Instead of questioning me or anything like that, she burst into laughter! She was laughing so hard that she stood up to breathe and began walking around the porch, slapping her sides as if to make herself stop. She had an infectious laugh, so before I knew it, I joined in. I wanted to be mad at her for not getting it, but I couldn't help myself. In fact, I started laughing so hard that I fell down the porch steps. Before I could get up, the rest of family showed up at the door to see what was happening. Before Grandma could ask what was happening, she started to laugh herself. With that, Grandpa and Uncle Frank joined in the chorus.

For a brief moment, I imagined what someone might think if they drove by right at that time and saw us all hysterically laughing on the porch. What a sight! Eventually, we began to calm down, and I started to breathe again. I realized that the adults would want to know what this was all about. I figured, rather than getting into it, I would end the discussion right there.

"Boy, Megan. I got you good!"

Right on cue, she chimed in, "You sure did. I forgot how goofy you really are!"

Thankfully, Grandma took the bait. "Oh, the joy of youth! I remember being silly like that once," she replied with a big grin.

But for some reason, when I looked at Uncle Frank, he had a different look. There was something about his expression that told me he thought there was more to it. I had no idea how he could possibly suspect anything.

"Well, laughing really makes you hungry. And I can't wait to have some chicken pot pie! Let's eat."

It worked; everyone turned their attention to food, and into the dinner table we went. The conversation didn't return to the cause of the front porch giggles, but the dinner was filled with a lot of laughter that night—and some very delicious chicken pot pies!

The Revelation

Grandma still makes the best chicken pot pies! I could have eaten two if I didn't have to save room for dessert. It was while Grandpa was clearing dishes and Grandma was getting dessert that I was put on the spot. There was something about the look on Uncle Frank's face on the porch that made me know he wasn't going to let this go. And his look wasn't his usual look of joking around. It was almost as if he *knew.*

"So, Billy, what was all that laughter about anyway? You guys were really going!"

Grandpa stopped clearing the dishes and chimed in too. "Yes. What was so funny?"

Before I could say anything, Megan answered their questions. "Billy was up to his old tricks. He was trying to convince me that he saw something when he was flying here. He made up this whole thing about seeing somebody in the clouds! Imagine that. What did you say, Billy? Cloud person?"

Now I was getting nervous. I was afraid I was going to be embarrassed. I even started questioning myself. Maybe I did just imagine the whole thing. After all, it was pretty ridiculous—no, impossible. While all this was running through my head, I looked over at Uncle Frank. He was looking directly back at me. He had a weird expression. I was so used to Uncle Frank being Uncle Frank. I never saw him looking like that. He then glanced over at Grandpa who had not only stopped clearing the table but sat down. I never imagined that I would hear what then came out of Uncle Frank's mouth. After looking at Grandpa, he was now looking at me.

"Cloud people. You saw one, did you?"

There was something about the way he said it. It wasn't typical Uncle Frank. Something was up, and why was he looking at Grandpa the way he did? Again, the look on his face told me this wasn't one of his jokes. He was serious. And the way he asked the question made me think that somehow, he knew what I was talking about. How could that be? Was it possible? I don't know how I had the courage to ask, but I did.

"You've seen one, Uncle Frank? You actually know what I'm talking about?"

Uncle Frank didn't answer but gave a nodding smile and looked over at Grandpa at the same time. That's all I needed.

"So it was real! I knew it. I just knew it!" I could hardly contain himself. I stood up and started walking around the table, waving my hands. I just started talking. Now that I had an opening, I had to get it out! "I knew I'm not crazy. I can't get it out of my mind. I keep seeing that face. I can't stop thinking about it."

The more I talked, the more excited I got. The more excited I got, the faster I found myself circling the table. Finally, Uncle Frank jumped up. He grabbed my shoulders.

"It's okay. Relax. Please sit down. You're making me dizzy! We understand. I know what you're talking about. Just calm down. Let's have some dessert, and we can talk about it…without doing laps!"

I took a deep breath. My heart was pounding, and I was sweating. I realized how worked up I had become. I apologized, mostly to Grandma, for getting so carried away.

"It's okay, Billy. I was young once too. I'll tell you what. Megan and I will clear the table and get dessert ready. You boys can talk."

Megan instantly protested. Her curiosity was peaked, and she was not going to be left out. "Oh, Grandma (she called her Grandma too). Can't I stay at the table? I want to find out what's going on. I'll be happy to help later, but please let me stay?"

As if expecting the protest, Grandma, without complaint, relented. "Okay, Megan. Stay with the boys. I can handle the dishes by myself," she replied with an obvious attempt at pity.

I knew Megan, and there was *no* way she was going to miss out on this. She wanted in on this big mystery, and I wanted to know how Uncle Frank knew what I had seen. And as I thought about it, I realized that Grandpa didn't seem surprised at all. This was turning out to be quite a dinner! Before I could ask anything, Megan started.

"Uncle Frank, what's this all about? What are cloud people? Are they real? What are they?"

I wasn't about to let Megan ask the questions. After all, I was the one that saw one these things! I blurted out, "Hey, wait a minute. I'm the one that saw one. I'll ask the questions." I glanced over at Megan to make sure she would stay quiet.

"All right. Go ahead. I'll be quiet, Billy," she said in a way that let me know she wasn't pleased!

"So, Uncle Frank, what gives? Did you really see one?"

Both Megan and I looked intently at Uncle Frank in anticipation of his answer. It felt like one of those moments when everyone is waiting to open the envelope to hear the winner. "Well, Billy and Megan, before I answer, you should know that I'm not the only one who has seen them. Grandpa saw them years before I did. In fact, I felt exactly the same as you do right now, only that was twenty years ago. You see, I saw them while I was flying a mission in Vietnam. I couldn't tell anyone then. They would have thought I was crazy. I kept it to myself till I was discharged. I was right in this same house, and believe it or not, we were having chicken pot pies. I looked at Grandpa and asked if I could tell him something. I think he was expecting something from the war, but I told him what I saw. I was as stunned and relieved as you were just now when Grandpa not only told me he believed me but that he had seen them too. Yes, Billy, they are real."

"That is so cool!" Megan shouted out. "This is so unbelievable!"

There she went again, taking my thunder. Those were *my* lines!

"Wow. Thanks, Uncle Frank. I know what I saw, but I really thought that I only imagined the whole thing. I can't tell you what a relief this is. But if they're real, what are they?"

Before I got an answer, Megan jumped in again! "Grandma, what do you think? Did you know about these cloud people?"

"Yea, Grandma," I added, still not wanting Megan to have control of the conversation. "What do you think? Have you seen them? Do you believe?"

She sat down at the table next to me and smiled her best Grandma smile. "Relax, Billy. I know all about it. Your Grandpa and I have a great marriage. We don't have secrets. In fact, I was the first one he told. Yes, I know all about them, and yes, I do believe you."

Grandma always had a reassuring way about her. Okay. She believes me, and Uncle Frank and Grandpa have seen them, but what about Megan?

"Hey Megan. What about you? What do you think?"

I don't know why, but it was important to know that she believed me. She didn't answer right away. I was trying to read her mind. Her expression didn't give her away. What was she thinking? I just stared at her, waiting for the verdict. Finally, I couldn't wait anymore.

"Come on, Megan. You've got to believe us. I wouldn't make up something like this. Aren't we friends? I wouldn't pull a trick on you like this. You've got to believe me, I mean us."

"I believe you," she said with a smile on her face "I trust you, Billy, but I don't understand. What are cloud people? Where do they come from? Why haven't more people seen them? What did you really see?"

"I wish I could tell you. I don't know myself. It doesn't make sense, but I did see one, and somehow, so did Uncle Frank and Grandpa. All I know is that it had a face. It had eyes and even what looked like a mouth. Whatever it was, it looked like it was sleeping. Suddenly, it opened its eyes as if it was startled by the plane. He looked right at me, almost as if he was scared or worried that I had seen him. Suddenly, he was gone. I can't really say if he had a body. I was so focused on his face. I can't forget those eyes. They were so real and so clear. I mean, he looked right at me."

Uncle Frank, Grandpa, and even Grandma, just nodded their heads in assent, as if to say, "That's right."

Then I looked over at Megan and said, "Are you sure you believe too?"

She didn't answer but just looked at me as if to say, "I'm not sure."

Grandpa

Up to that moment, Grandpa didn't say anything but just kept nodding his approval. Finally, he joined the conversation, and I was glad he did. I wanted to know his story. He sat up in his chair and leaned forward toward Megan. He looked at her and gave her one of his famous big Grandpa smiles.

"You thought you were just coming for dinner, and now you're in the Twilight Zone!" His laughter brought a smile to Megan's face. "Until Billy brought up his experience tonight, I haven't spoken of this since Uncle Frank and I talked about it at this very table. I'm glad you and Billy are the first to hear. It is hard to grasp, but they are real. I know that as sure as you and I are sitting here. Yes. They're real all right."

With that, he began his incredible story. Grandma and Uncle Frank already knew, but my heart was pounding in anticipation. I looked over at Megan, and her eyes were glued to Grandpa, waiting to hear just like me.

"Like Uncle Frank, I saw my cloud people during the service. As you know, I was in the air force during the Korean War. I flew an F-86 Sabre Jet. The North Koreans had Russian Migs, but we got the best of them. I was pretty lucky, but one time, I almost 'bought it.' I had just been in a dogfight with a Mig, which I managed to knock out of the sky. Before I did though, he hit me. That was the first time I got shot. I heard a bang and felt my jet tilt. I managed to keep it straight and fire back with success. However, my jet was hit, and I started to spin. Not only that, but clouds had rolled in, and I became disoriented. The hit knocked out my radar, and I couldn't get my bearings. I didn't know where I was or where I was heading.

"Just as I started to panic, I saw it. There, right in front of my windshield, I saw a face, just like you saw Billy. It looked like a cloud, but it definitely had eyes and appeared to have a body. It blended in with the clouds, but it was definitely a face and a body! Well, I thought I must be seeing things. I began to wonder if I was shot and maybe even dying. I figured I had a serious wound and was hallucinating. Well, it was just at that moment that the thing, the face, looked right at me. He had a look, if I can say that about a cloud, of urgency. He started waving what I think was arms in a frantic motion, pointing to my right. He was like the guy at the airport directing the plane, except this thing was in hyper mode. He just kept doing it. I finally realized that whatever I was seeing was trying to communicate. It was telling me to turn my jet to my right. I don't know why I did, but I instinctively veered to the right. Just as I did, I heard a whooshing sound followed by another go right past me on my left. I glanced back and could hardly see anything in the clouds, but my wits were coming back. As my head cleared, I realized that I just missed two Russian Migs. I had avoided them, but the day wasn't over. They saw me and were turning around. They were coming to get me.

"Now I was really scared. I don't think my heart could have pounded any harder. If it did, it would have jumped out of my chest! I was completely focused on getting out of there and saving my neck. I wasn't even thinking about the cloud guy at all, but suddenly, there he was again. This time, he was pointing me to go left, with even greater energy than before. Just as I did so, he began pointing straight up. Again, I don't know why I did, but I did exactly as he was telling me. In a flash, I was in the clear, and I could finally see where I was. But that wasn't the end of it. I still can't believe what happened next.

"As I flew off to escape, I managed to glance back. When I did—I still can't believe it—I saw what looked like a whole bunch of cloud people following me. There were more faces than I could count, and they were following me. Then I realized what they were doing. These things, these cloud people, were actually creating cover for me! They formed a huge bank of clouds that were blocking the Migs from seeing me. I'm sure they still had radar, but they couldn't see me. Suddenly, the mass of what looked like a bunch of cloud faces got darker and darker. As the mass of clouds got blacker and blacker, I couldn't see the faces anymore—except one. His face was right in the middle, sticking out from the rest. From beside his face, I saw a kind of arm reach out with a hand that was pointing downward. After seeing that, the face disappeared, and there was a flash of lightning. There was a rumble of thunder, and the clouds became even darker. I was mesmerized for a moment by the whole thing but suddenly shook my head to snap myself out of it. I was still in the middle of a war and in a battle for my life. Once again, without even thinking, I did exactly what the face told me do. I took a sharp dive. After a short distance, I was out of the cloud cover and could see that the Migs were above me and to my left. I had the element of surprise on my side and didn't waste any time. I stalled the engine, fell behind the Migs, then flew upward on their tails. I started blasting. I wanted to hit them before they realized what was happening. That's exactly what happened. I got them both! I still can't believe how accurate I was. Well, with smoke coming out, they fell to the ground like two rocks. With that, I got out of there as fast as I could. I didn't wanted look for any more Migs and certainly no more trouble.

"As I sped away back to base, I turned my jet slightly to the side to take one last look back. Those cloud things were well behind me now, but they were still there—the clouds that literally saved my life. I couldn't see any faces from that distance. I still wasn't sure what I saw, but I know I didn't imagine it. Whatever it was, it was real. Otherwise, I know I wouldn't be here to tell the story. Well, I was one lucky pilot that day. As I continued my flight back and as I was thinking about what happened, well, I couldn't help myself. I quickly looked around to make sure there was no one around, even though I knew there wasn't, and I made a quick salute in the direction of those fading clouds. Then I dipped my wing to say, 'Thank You,' just in case they could still see me."

With that Grandpa put his face in his hands and started to cry. He wasn't loud or anything, but I could see the tears rolling down his face. Uncle Frank got up and put his hands on his shoulders. As another veteran, I guess he just understood. No one talked for a few minutes. It was a powerful moment. I still get chills when I think about it.

After a few moments, he wiped his face and sat up. He took a deep breath and continued. "I can't explain what I saw, but I know what I saw, and I know what happened—and what could have happened. I was very, very lucky that day. Yes, I'm a blessed man. I was super lucky that day."

There was silence at the table as Grandpa stopped talking. I just sat there with my mouth open. I'm not sure if I was just shocked at the story or still couldn't believe that someone else actually saw what I saw. I looked over at Megan. She had some tears running down her face. She got up and went over to give Grandpa a hug. After a moment, Grandpa seemed to compose himself. He smiled at Megan.

She sat down and he continued. "Believe it or not, there's more to the story! When I got out of my jet, I was met by the other pilots. They were high-fiving and hugging me. They all said they were so glad to see me. Then one pilot, Pete, spoke for the rest. 'How did you get out of there? When we saw all those Migs, we got out of there as fast as we could. We thought you were with us, but then when we checked, you were nowhere to be found.'

"'I told them, 'Well, thanks for leaving me behind. It was pretty scary being outnumbered two to one, but I managed to hide behind some clouds and get away.' Then came the really shocking part. Pete just looked at me and laughed. 'Yea, right,' he said. 'Two to one. If that's all there was, all of us would have stayed. Pal, there were at least ten Migs up there.' 'Are you kidding me?' I asked. 'Are you serious? That's impossible. I only saw two.' 'Well, Frank, I didn't take an actual count, but it was at least ten. Right, guys?' he said, looking to the others for confirmation. They all nodded in agreement. From the looks on their faces, it was obvious that they meant it. We flew a lot of missions together, so we knew each other pretty well. No. They were not joking. Ten! I still can't believe it. Ten Migs, and here I am to talk about it."

I knew Grandpa wasn't making it up, but this was getting really bizarre. First, I find out that others saw what I did, and now I hear that they saved my grandfather's life. What are these things? Do they think? Do they watch over us? I had a million questions. Finally, I just started firing them at Grandpa.

"So, Grandpa, what are they? What could they be? How can they exist? Where do they come from?"

Before Grandpa could answer, Uncle Frank jumped in. "Well, Billy, I know they're real, but I can't explain them. There are a lot of things in nature we can't explain. Take armadillos, for instance. There is as weird an animal as you'll find. Where do they come from? Over the years, creatures have evolved, adapted, changed. Personally, I think these cloud things have been around a long time. They must have come out of the water and evolved into sky creatures, while other animals moved out of the water and on to the land. Beyond that, I have no idea. We can't explain them, but they are real, just like armadillos!"

"Well, since you're my nephew, I'm not going to argue religion with you again," Grandpa said with a smile.

He knew Uncle Frank well, and over the years, they had many discussions about life and God and what it's all about. Uncle Frank was all science. He didn't go much for religion. I guess it's the way he grew up, losing his dad at a young age. Mom always said that generation had a lot of questions. The whole Vietnam War, which I still don't get, messed up his mind, she would say. Still she loved her older cousin. I liked Uncle Frank too. Odd as he was, he was still a great guy.

Grandpa, on the other hand, was quite religious. He went to Mass every week, read the Bible, and prayed faithfully every day. He was a very good man, and he saw God's hand in just about everything. Even though he had a strong faith, he wasn't one to argue, although I think he enjoyed getting into it with Uncle Frank. Over the years, they had many good-natured debates, and tonight I could tell was going to be another. They loved to rib each other. Grandpa took a sip of coffee and gave me a wink.

"Well, Frank, there you go again. You know how I feel about all that evolution nonsense. I just don't see how this complicated world could be an accident. It's all so beautiful, and everything has a place, yes, armadillos, and even you, Frank," he added as he took another sip of coffee with a smile on his face. "Now me, I've always figured these cloud people are kind of like guardian angels. Like everything God created, they have a purpose. I know they were my angels that day in the sky. I can't explain them, but I think, somehow, they're a gift from God. After all, there's so much about this world that we don't know. That's part of the problem with science. We think we can know it all, and we forget that life can be a mystery, and that's beautiful. I think believing only in science takes all the fun out of life."

"Pops, (that's what he usually called his uncle), you know I love you. I have the greatest respect for you, but we've been down this road before," Uncle Frank said with a polite smile. "I'm not going to get into all that now. Besides, it's getting rather late."

"Okay," Grandpa conceded, but he couldn't resist a final word. "I know you're not that big on all that religious stuff and the Bible, but for me, I can't help but think of when God saved His people through Moses. A column of clouds protected the Israelites from the Egyptians when they crossed the Red Sea. God used them for His purpose. Just like God used clouds back in the Bible, I think He used them for me that day. I don't care what you say. To me, they're like angels. They were sent by God!"

Just then, their religious debate was interrupted by the sound of snoring. Megan was sound asleep! I looked at the clock and saw that it was two thirty in the morning. No wonder she was asleep. I almost nodded off a few times, but I enjoyed Grandpa and Uncle Frank's discussion. Each time they went at it, I always wondered who would win. I guess the suspense kept me awake!

Realizing the time, Uncle Frank said, "Wow. I had no idea it was that late. I guess it's time for bed. But wait a minute!" Just then, he realized that Megan's parents must be wondering where she was. In a panic, he jumped up to go the phone.

With perfect timing, Grandma came in with a big grin. She stopped Uncle Frank before he could get to the phone. "Don't worry. I already took care of it. Hours ago, I could tell you would keep Megan up till late, so I already made arrangements for her to sleep here tonight. The spare bedroom is all set. In fact, her folks said she can stay for the week. I'm way ahead of you."

She seemed to take great delight in letting Uncle Frank know that she was ahead of the game. Uncle Frank just smiled back and then gave her a hug.

"You always take care of everyone. You're the best. Well, since you have everything under control, I'm going to bed!"

With that, Grandpa gently stirred Megan, telling her that it was time to go to bed. "Megan, Grandma called your parents, and they said that not only can you stay tonight, but you can stay for the week! The spare bedroom is all set."

That news perked her up as she jumped up off her seat. She loved to stay with my grandparents, even though she didn't live far away. She had been a guest many times and knew the spare bedroom quite well. This was indeed an unexpected treat. Her excitement though was temporarily interrupted.

"But wait, I didn't bring anything. I can't stay. I have to go home."

Once again, Grandma came to the rescue. "Don't worry. I've already taken care of that too. While all of you had your head in the clouds, I went to your house and got a bag." With that, she produced the results of her planning and handed it to Megan. "Okay, everyone, that's it. Now let's get to bed before the sun comes up!"

However, as the one who always had to get in a last word, even as late as it was, Uncle Frank walked out on the porch and quickly came back in.

"Well, gang. That's strange. After all this talk about clouds, it's clear as a bell tonight. Not a cloud in sight."

I didn't have the energy for any comeback. Part of me didn't want the day to end, but it was time to go to bed. I don't think I even had the energy to make it up the stairs. Finally, the decision was made for me.

Uncle Frank came over, scooped me up, and declared, "You're going to bed!"

Even though I was certainly old enough to put myself to bed, I was exhausted. Uncle Frank was a strong man, and he lifted me as if I was pillow. I felt silly being carried, but I was also glad I didn't have to walk up the steps. When he got to my room, he dumped me on the bed.

"Good night. See you in the morning."

I barely managed to get into my pajamas and was soon fast asleep—but my night was about to begin!

The Dream—or Was It?

I guess it goes along with my fascination with clouds, but I have always wondered what it would be like to fly. So many times, when I look up at the sky, I daydream about soaring above the trees. Well, I was shocked, for as soon as I closed my eyes that first night of my vacation, even though I was really beat, I opened my eyes, and I was floating in the air above my grandparents' house! I could see the tops of the trees in their yard and the surrounding area. I was flying! I couldn't believe it. I was actually flying. When I went to sleep, I was exhausted, but now I was not only wide awake but flying in the air above my grandparent's house!

At first, a feeling of panic came over me. I started to think about what was happening. How am I up here? Is this a dream? What's keeping me up? What if I fall? I began flapping my arms frantically like a bird figuring I had nothing to lose. As I did that, and I still can't believe it, I began to move through the air. I didn't know how, but it gradually sunk in that I was flying, and I wasn't going to fall. It totally felt like what I always imagined a bird must feel! Slowly, I started getting the hang of this flying business. It took a little while to get over all my fear, but soon I was swooping and diving and, in between, soaring—just like the birds. Before too long, it felt as easy to me as walking. This was fun!

As my confidence grew, I started to experiment with my new-found ability. I descended to just above some trees and held my hands out as I skimmed over the branches. It was an awesome feeling to let the leaves pass through my fingers as I glided along. After a couple of runs at the tops of the trees, I really got daring. I began to dart in between the trees and even the branches. I wondered just how close I could get. With each dive through the trees, I started looking for more and more challenging openings. There were a couple of close calls, but each time, I soared right through without a scratch. I was getting good!

After flying around for I don't know how long, I began to look around me. Of course, I could see my grandparent's house and yard, but I also saw some of the houses in the distance. Some had lights on, but most were dark. I even heard a dog barking in the distance. If I wanted to, I could have flown over to where I heard the sound was coming from to see what was happening. The world was really fascinating at night, and I had it all to myself.

I was taking all this in when the thought occurred to me that there was something else I always wanted to do. So many times, I used to envy birds sitting on top of a tree or a wire or a house and looking down at the world. Sometimes in school, when I looked out the window at the clouds, I would see a bird perched on top of a tree. One time, I got so caught up in imagining what that would be like, I got in trouble. The teacher busted me for daydreaming. Well, now I didn't have a teacher watching me, and I didn't have to imagine any longer. I'm going to do it! I'm going perch someplace and just sit there and take it all in. All I had to do was find the perfect spot. It didn't take long—there it was. Not too far from my grandparents' house was a water tower. It wasn't as cool as the trees, but it was high. I wanted to find the highest spot so I could get a good look around. Yup. That's where I was going. It was the perfect place. I flapped my wings, I mean my arms, and flew up to the top of the tower. I landed so soft and easy—and there I was!

I'm not sure how long I sat there, but it was so peaceful and calm. I lost track of time. Suddenly, I noticed that the sun was starting to come up! I couldn't believe it. Had I really been up all night? And I wasn't even tired. I said to myself that I probably should get back to my room before I was missed, but I couldn't resist one more spin in the air. As I lifted up off the bell tower, the sun was coming up on the horizon, and everything was so beautiful. I don't think I had ever experienced anything so amazing. As I floated peacefully through the air, I suddenly realized all the clouds around me. I guess because it was dark, I hadn't seen them through the night, and besides, I was just so thrilled at being able to fly. But there they were, and the sight of them practically took my breath away. How many times had I looked out the window at school and daydreamed about doing what I was now doing—floating with the clouds!

I began to study them. I was fascinated at how many shapes and designs there were. Up close, they were even more incredible than when I looked at them from the ground. After studying them, it occurred to me that I could now fulfill another fantasy. I could fly into the clouds. I had seen planes do that many times, but now was my chance. I plunged into the nearest cloud formation and rotated my body so I could look around. It was like being in a fog. I couldn't really see anything, but it was still so cool to be flying around inside a cloud!

Just when I thought my experience couldn't get any better, it happened. Out of nowhere, I began to hear voices. I was still floating among the clouds, and I know there was nothing or no one around me, but I definitely heard voices. It sounded like people talking and laughing, but I couldn't tell where the sound was coming from. I started darting in and out of the clouds, trying to discover the source of the talking. What was I hearing? Where were the voices coming from? After all, I was flying in the air all by myself. What could it be?

Thinking that I might be going crazy, I decided that I should forget about it. That's when I heard it, one distinct and clear voice, "Come closer."

I spun my head around in all directions but still couldn't see anything. I know I heard it. It was unmistakable. Then the voice came again, even louder, "It's okay. Come over."

Over? Over where? I moved in the direction of the voice, leaving one bunch of clouds and entering another. Then I saw it. Right in front of me was one face among many smiling faces, faces in the clouds. And along with the faces were countless hands waving at me! They all looked so friendly, and everyone was giggling. It reminded me of the laughter of the munchkins in the *Wizard of Oz*.

I froze in midair. I wasn't flapping my arms or anything but remained in one spot, floating right in front of all those faces. I looked at them in wonder, and they looked at me. I don't know how long I stayed there, but I still couldn't believe what I was seeing. I was fascinated and continued to survey the faces in front of me. They pretty much all looked the same, but some faces were small, some large, some had big eyes, some small. The one thing I could tell from looking at them is that they were all friendly.

Then it hit me. Cloud people! These are cloud people! This is what I saw from the plane, and here I am right in front of not just one but dozens and dozens of them. Wow. Real live cloud people! Once I realized what I was looking at and what was happening, I asked myself again if this was real. Was I dreaming? Am I asleep? I felt wide awake, so I figured this couldn't be a dream. I felt the air around me; the sun was coming up, and it was getting warmer. It was all so real, but how was that possible?

It felt like time stopped. For a moment, I thought I might be in heaven, but then I said that there's no way that could be. So what is this? What happens now? Do I speak? Will one of them speak again? Then it hit me. I never really *heard* voices. What I heard was in my head. It's weird, but it wasn't like sound travelling through the air and hitting my ears. It was more like thoughts in my head. It was as if they were communicating thoughts. If they're sending me thoughts, how was I supposed to "talk" to them? What next? As I was wondering what to do, one of them "spoke." I will never forget those words.

We have been waiting to meet you.

As stunning as that invitation was, what happened next was even more amazing. I was trying to figure out what to say. I was thinking to myself, *Wow. That's great, but I don't know what's happening. I don't know what to do now.*

As those thoughts raced through my head, the cloud responded, *It's okay. I can understand you.*

What? I hadn't said anything, but the cloud guy knew what I was thinking. Was he reading my mind?

Relax. Relax. It's really no different than talking. Just think your thoughts, and I will understand. It's not that difficult.

I still don't know how I did it, but somehow, I was able to communicate. It was such an odd feeling, but just as I learned to fly, I started "talking" to the clouds. Within moments, I poured out a ton of questions.

You've been waiting to meet me? Where have you been? How do you know me? Did you see me on the plane?

It's a good thing I was thinking my thoughts because if I was talking, my lips wouldn't have been able to keep up! Finally, the one cloud that was in the center of all of the others put up his hand and, with a big smile, said, *Okay. Okay. Slow it down. Please. We're excited to meet you, but you're going to give me what in your world is a head-ache, but for me, I guess that's a cloud ache!*

As soon as he said that, we were surrounded by laughter. Every one of the clouds was laughing hysterically. It was infectious. I started laughing right along with them. I was almost laughing as hard as I did on the porch when I first told Megan about seeing one of these cloud people. I slowly stopped and began to breathe again. That outburst was just what I needed. It calmed me down. I took a deep breath and waited for all the clouds to also stop laughing. At last, there was calm again.

This time my thoughts were more controlled. I was going to take it one question at a time. Starting all over, I said, *My name is Billy. What's yours?*

Well, said the lead cloud person with a smile, *that's much better. My name is Zon. I'm the leader of this group of clouds. You see, each cluster of clouds has a leader. My cluster is quite small compared to a lot of them, but I think we have some of the nicest clouds around! I'm glad we were the first to meet you. It was one of our group that saw you on the plane yesterday. Ever since, we've been hoping to meet you.*

I knew it. I knew I saw one of you guys on the plane. Gosh, I don't mean, "one of you guys." Well, you know what I mean. That face, Zon's face, just smiled. *It's weird,* I said. *I just met you, and I feel so comfortable. I feel like I've always known you. In fact, you even remind me a little of my Grandpa.*

That's an honor. We think the world of your Grandpa.

What did you say? How can that be? You know my Grandpa? How can you possibly know him? How old are you anyway?

Zon let out a big belly laugh, the kind I imagine Santa Claus would have. After a pause, Zon said, *Well, that's a good question. I'm* not sure I can answer it in a way that you would understand. *Let's just say I've been around a while. In fact, I'm a lot older than your Grandpa.*

So you were there that day? He just told us a story of how you cloud people, I mean you saved his life during the war. That's true? You were there? Was that you? Zon again just looked at me with a big smile. He didn't say anything. *Okay. I get it. You're old. You were there. But I really don't get it. How can that be? I mean what are you? What you are you made out of? Where did you come from? How come people don't know about you?* I tried to hold back. I didn't want to be rude and certainly didn't want to overwhelm my new friend, but I couldn't help myself. I was right back at rattling off an endless list of questions. I had to know the answers. *I always thought that you, I mean clouds, were mostly air.*

Well, Billy, did you know that you are mostly water? That's right, more than half. You feel solid, but you have a lot of water floating around inside of you. I guess we just take it to a slightly higher level! It was funny, but he made the point. I was beginning to understand—a little. *You see, didn't you learn that God made you out of clay, out of the dirt. Well, God did the same with us, except He used clouds, water, and air. If He can form you out of dust, why can't He make us out of clouds?* After a pause, Zon couldn't resist continuing, *So what that means, Billy, is that you're mostly dirt, and we're mostly all air!*

I had to laugh. I remember thinking, *That was a good one.* Not only were Zon and I smiling, but all the clouds were beaming with delight.

I was beginning to understand a little, but I still had so many questions. I picked up right where I left off. *Do you have a family? I mean, is it the same as us made-of-dirt humans?*

With a big smile, Zon answered. *Yes. I have what you call a wife, but we call it something different. We believe that two clouds are meant to be together for all eternity and meant to stay together, so we call each other our* destiny. *My destiny is Bon. She's beautiful. She's not here right now, but I would love for you to meet her.*

Wow, I said. *That's kind of cool. But I do have to ask one thing about that. Please don't get upset, but I don't understand how you can say that Bon is beautiful. I mean all of you, now don't get upset, all you cloud people pretty much look the same!*

Zon and all the clouds burst into laughter. I wasn't trying to be funny, and I didn't want to hurt my new friend's feelings. I just had to know. At least their laughing let me know that I hadn't offended them.

After a pause, Zon looked at me with a huge grin. *You think that we look alike. I'm sorry to tell you, Billy, but you should see yourself through our eyes. I think the only reason you humans grow hair is so that you can tell each other apart. Seriously, take away the hair, and you're mostly the same.* That reply earned another burst of laughter through the clouds. I never thought of it that way, but I had to admit he had a point.

At that moment, I was beginning to feel like I do when my family gets together over the summer for a barbecue or picnic. We were having such a good time, when all of a sudden and without any warning, it started to get dark. All the clouds also noticed and began to look worried. Then off in the distance, I heard the rumble of thunder. Of course, I've heard thunder many times before, but this was different. It was right next to me. It felt like there was a freight train coming down the tracks, and I was standing in the way! Just a moment before, I was filled with excitement at my great discovery, but now I was really getting scared and didn't know what to do. I was entering panic mode when I started to think things through. I started telling myself that these are only clouds around me. They are made of air and water. What's the worst that can happen? Maybe I'll get a little wet. I might even like that.

Just as I talked myself into staying calm, I heard Zon booming in my head. *Get out of here, Billy. You've got to move,* now!"

With that, Zon and the other cloud people vanished. I was left dangling there, all alone, and now super scared—for real! Still, I didn't move. I was floating in the air, and I couldn't budge. I felt paralyzed. As I was trying to figure out what to do, my thoughts were interrupted as I again heard Zon screaming in my head, *Move now!*

With that, I instinctively flew up higher as if I was leaping out of the way of a charging bull. As I did so, the thought crossed my mind that I probably should have just gone back down to the ground, but now it was too late.

Now right below me, I could see a mass of black clouds, and things were getting turbulent. It felt as if I was on the edge of a great battle. All I could think of was one of those scenes from *Lord of the Rings* when the orcs stormed the castle. It was pretty intense. I couldn't see anything or anyone, but it was so loud I put my hand over my ears. Just as I was doing that, I saw sparks of light in the clouds, what I guessed were flashes of lighting. Thinking that I might get shocked or electrocuted or something, I figured I better move up even higher. The flashes were just below my feet, and I could feel splashes of water coming out of the clouds. There was a strong wind, and I was suddenly being bounced around like a balloon. I couldn't get away, and now I was sure that I was going to die.

This can't be happening! I kept saying to myself. *Zon, where are you? Help! Help!*

I don't think I had ever been so scared in my life. I was terrified and felt helpless. Here I was, stuck at the edge of this raging storm, and there was no way out. I remember thinking that there's no way this can get any worse, when sure enough, it did. Not only was I hearing the rumble and dodging sparks, but now, I started hearing voices. They sounded angry and aggressive. I was in the middle of a shouting match except I couldn't see anybody or anything. I was surrounded by yelling and screaming. Gradually, I began to make out some of the of the words, and they were awful. It was more than arguing. It was pure hate. I heard, *You're no good! Get out of my way! I hate you! I'm going to get rid of you! You can't stop me!*

I was still freaking out when something inside of me told me to look up. I'm not sure why I obeyed that instinct, but I was desperate. As I did, I was relieved to see my new friend Zon just out of range of the storm. He had a look of concern, and the words he spoke to me were not a suggestion but an order.

Get up here, now!

The tone of his command and the look on his face shook me out of my paralysis. In a blink, I darted straight up and found myself next to Zon. He didn't give me any chance to relax but grabbed my hand and pulled me away from that chaos, whatever it was.

For a while, I just floated there, grateful to be with Zon and finally safe. After I composed myself, I asked him, *What's going on? What was that all about?*

Before answering, Zon came closer to me and placed his cloud hand on my shoulder. I could barely feel it, but I knew it was there.

He just looked at me with such compassion for a while and then finally asked, *Are you all right?*

Well, yea. Sure. I was frightened at first, then I thought it was cool, but then I got scared again—actually really scared. Anyway, it's over, so yea, sure, I'm okay.

Good, said Zon. *That's good. I'm glad you're okay. You see, that happens too often, and we never get used to it. Every now and then, a fight erupts. That was a bad one. Those guys have been at each other for as long as I can remember. That's what you saw and felt.*

What do you mean a fight? I didn't see anybody. I didn't see any fighting. You mean clouds fight? How do they fight? Not for nothing, but seriously, how much can a cloud punch hurt?

Zon smiled and then tried to explain. *Up here, things happen a little differently. We don't fight like you humans do. When anyone has a disagreement or has something like what you would call angry or hurt feelings, bad energy builds up. When that bad energy has no place to go, it continues to grow and becomes dark. If others join in the anger, it builds up even more, and that negative energy gets darker and darker. If it doesn't have a way to scatter, it finally explodes. You know that as thunder. You see, the energy has to be discharged. It has to be gotten rid of. When that discharge is really big, if there's a large buildup of bad energy, it comes out as lightning. That's bad.*

So let me get this straight. When you guys fight, you only think about it, but don't actually fight?

Basically, that's right, Billy. You got it.

I guess that's good, but it does seem a little weird. But wait a minute. I guess I can get the whole bad energy thing, but seriously, what do you have to fight about. You're all just floating around, living the easy life. How could anybody get mad?

Well, most of the time it's over space under the sun. Clouds will fight for the best spots.

Are you serious? I asked. *That's ridiculous. There's plenty of room for everyone. Just move over and pick another spot. I'm sorry, Zon, but that's ridiculous.*

Ridiculous? Seriously. You're telling me you don't get it? Do you know anything about your history? Look at all the wars that have been fought for just the same reason. And you think what we fight about is silly? he said as he gave me a challenging look.

I could see that Zon had a lot of wisdom. Now I was afraid that maybe I had upset him and all the clouds. I didn't want to hurt him during our first meeting. It's just that I was trying to understand. I felt so bad.

Hey, Zon. Look. I'm sorry. I don't know what I'm saying. I didn't mean anything by that. I'm just trying to figure all this out. But now that I think about, I have to admit that we humans do fight about a lot of stupid stuff. It's funny, but it's not until you take a look at yourself from the outside that you can understand how dumb it all is. You're right. We fight as much as you do, probably more. Maybe we could learn something from you clouds.

Well, Zon added, *maybe we can learn from each other.* He reached out with his cloud hand and patted me on the head. *I have always thought that all fights are ridiculous.* Then almost as if it was planned, I could hear the faint rumble of thunder, or rather the fighting that had just passed, off in the distance. I was still trying to absorb this whole new world, and I still had a lot of questions. I was about to ask another when I noticed that all of the cloud people were coming back. It reminded me of when people finally start going back outside after it stops raining.

With a big crowd of faces, now instead of having a conversation with just Zon, I felt as if I was on stage. Now I was in front of a huge audience. I was still trying to get a hold of this new reality, and there was so much I wanted to understand. Feeling put on the spot, I was almost going to let my next question go, but I couldn't.

Zon, look, I just saw what happens when you guys get mad—

Before I could continue, Zon interrupted. *Well, not all thunder, lightning, and storms are because of a fight. Sometimes, it happens for other reasons.*

Okay, but I was wondering what happens when it's all over. I mean, I saw the darkness. I heard the thunder. But now it's all gone. It's getting bright, and slowly the sun is coming out. Where did it all go? I mean what happened to those clouds? Where are they? Did they just disappear? What happens to you?

Zon waited a few minutes and my curiosity was building.

At last, he spoke. *For you on the ground, I know when you don't see us anymore, it looks like we went away. That's one of the cool things about being vapor. We can change form. No, we don't disappear. We're still around. It's just that we, I guess you could say, become invisible. We're still there, doing all the things we normally do, but you can't see us.*

Are you kidding me, Zon? Is that true? Then after I thought for a second, I added, *But if that is true, can you see each other? I mean, what do you see? What do you look like when you're invisible?* As soon as I said that I realized how dumb it sounded.

Zon continued, *No, Billy, I'm not kidding you. That really is the way it is with us. And yes, we can still see each other. It's kind of hard to explain, but for us, we see each other as plainly on a bright sunny day as you can see us now. Right at this moment, you can see us as white and puffy. At other times, we can be black or gray and, other times, even orange or red.*

Wow, this is getting complicated. So you're telling me that on a clear day when there isn't a cloud in the sky, you guys are still up here, and you can see each other just like you do now... I just don't get it. I believe you, but I just don't get it.

That's okay, Billy. There's a lot of things we don't understand about your world either! As he said that, I must have gotten a strange look on my face because he then asked me, *What's this about school?*

He must have read my mind that I had a sudden flashback to my school. I don't know what brought that on, but it just popped into my head. I was thinking of those times I got bored learning about clouds, and here I was filled with curiosity. All I wanted to do was learn.

You know, Zon, I don't do that great in school. If I don't understand or don't like something, I get bored.

What are you trying to tell me, Billy? he asked.

I think I want to say thank you. Meeting you and asking all these questions actually makes me want to learn. I mean I never thought of finding out about the world as, well, cool.

I think that's great, Zon said. *We cloud people have something like your school. But to be honest, we love to learn. In fact, that's why we know so much about you, I mean human beings. All clouds learn about you and, of course, a lot of other stuff. For us, it's interesting. We love school.*

I must admit, I said to him, *I never thought of school that way. I guess I have a lot to learn about you, and I have a lot to learn about life. School actually being fun? I have to think about that a little more!* Zon just smiled.

Just then, I realized that it was really starting to get light. I had literally been "up" all night, and I didn't feel the least bit tired. I was as fresh and awake as I have ever been. I didn't want that night to end. I thought of all the times I had daydreamed about doing exactly this, floating in the clouds, and here I was. And not only that, I was actually talking with the clouds! Unbelievable, but how can I ever tell anyone? They'd all think I was nuts. I knew Uncle Frank would never let me live this down. I didn't know if even Megan would believe me. I had to put that aside for now because it really was getting light, and I had better get back to my room. Yup, even though I wanted to stay, I knew it was time to go.

I looked at Zon. *It has been so great meeting you. Thank you. Thank you. Thank you. This has been so amazing. I really don't want to go, but I should get back. If they don't see me in bed, my family will worry. I wish I could stay. I really do wish I could stay.*

As soon as I said those words, I couldn't help it. I started to cry. I just had the greatest experience of my life. I met some new friends that I didn't think I could ever tell anybody about, and now it's coming to an end. Will I ever see them again? The more I thought about it, the more I cried. Just then, Zon came over and gave me the biggest, warmest hug. His touch was light, but I could feel it, and

I could feel the love coming from him. It was as if he understood everything I was feeling. He was so comforting.

As he was helping me to feel better, the thought suddenly popped into my head. I started saying to myself, *Wait a minute! I'm probably the first person, maybe the only person, that has met and talked with the cloud people! I can't believe this. Here I am hugging one of them, floating above my grandparents' house. This is historic.*

Yet what was most important to me at that moment was saying goodbye to new friends. I felt as if I had known Zon all my life and now I have to go and I didn't know if I would ever see him again. To make matters worse, as I looked at Zon's face, I realized he was crying too. In that powerful moment, I could care less about making history or science or any of that. All I cared about was my friend... and our friendship.

Then I remembered that there were a lot of other clouds around us. As I gently pushed back from Zon, I could see that many of the other clouds also had tears in their eyes. I don't know why I thought of this then, but I'm glad I did because it helped break the sadness.

Wait a minute, Zon, I said. *Rain? Is this how it rains—I mean from all the tears?*

Zon wiped some tears from his eyes and allowed a beautiful smile to come across his face. As his smile grew, he looked at me and said, *No, Billy. That's not how it rains. We don't have enough tears to make that much water. Sorry, but it rains because moisture builds up among the clouds. We're above the rain, so we don't get wet. But if we want, from time to time, we can join the rain, but that's for another time. That's too much to explain right now.*

With those words, I forgot about my sadness and now started to become curious again. What did he mean by that? Before I start thinking about that, I realized I really had better get going. I had to go then, but something inside of me told me this really wasn't goodbye. Somehow, I knew I would see Zon and my friends again. So I gave him one last big hug. This time, it was more a hug of gratitude and friendship. As soon as I put my arms around him, I fell fast asleep. The long night had finally caught up with me.

That Morning

The next thing I heard was a low buzzing sound. I slowly opened my eyes and looked around. I was in my bed at my grandparents' house, and the sun was up. I hopped out of bed and ran to look out the window. The sky looked clear in the early morning, not a cloud in sight. I was surprised after last night's adventure at how awake I was. I didn't feel sleepy or exhausted or anything like that. I felt like I had the best sleep ever. I couldn't believe it, but I was wide awake.

Then I started thinking about what happened last night. Was it real? Was it a dream? What was that? I'd had dreams before, but they were never that real, and I could never remember all of it. I could only call to mind a bit here and a bit there. But last night, it was so vivid and real. I could remember *everything*. It couldn't have been only a dream, but how was that possible? I mean Grandpa and Uncle Frank said they had seen cloud people. They believed that's what I saw on the plane, so why couldn't it be real? Yes. It was real. It had to be. Yes, it had to be.

As I tried to decide whether the whole thing was real or not, I thought of Megan. I had to talk to her. Wait till she hears this! Then I realized, "Oh boy. Here we go again." It was enough to tell her about the plane ride, but now this. For sure she's going to think that I'm joking this time. At least before, I had Grandpa and Uncle Frank to back me up. Will she believe me this time? Right then, I didn't care. I knew what I experienced last night, and I had to tell her.

I was so distracted that I didn't even know what time it was. It seemed like it was still early, so I tried to be as quiet as I could when I opened my bedroom door. I slowly walked to Megan's room and was glad to see that her door was slightly open. As I peeked through the crack of her open door, I could see her lying in bed, but her eyes were open. She was awake! Good. Okay, here it goes…

"Megan, are you awake?"

I obviously startled her, but she sat up in bed and said, "Well, kind of. I was just lying here waiting for everyone else to get up."

"Good. I need to talk to you. I mean, I *really* need to talk to you."

With that, she looked straight into my eyes, "What's the matter?"

"Well, nothing's the matter, but I have to tell you something. You're not going to believe it."

"Really, Billy. It's too early for games. Are you playing games with me? It's too early." I guess the look on my face told her that I had something important on my mind because she relented. "Okay. I'm sorry. What is it Billy? Tell me."

Without thinking, I just started talking. I couldn't believe the words that were coming out of my mouth. "I was flying last night, Megan. I mean I was really flying. I was up there," I said as I pointed out her window. "I was flying!"

For a moment, Megan just stared at me. I could almost see her mind working. She was trying to figure out if I was just goofing with her or if I meant it. I couldn't blame her. Seriously. What would I think if she told me she went flying last night?

I don't know what she really thought, but I was glad that at least she didn't laugh at me. I kept studying her face, trying to guess which way she was leaning. I don't know how long we sat there looking at each other, trying to figure out what the other was thinking.

Finally, she spoke. "Really? Well, what was it like?"

The way she asked the question made me think she thought I was making it up. I wish she had believed me right away, but seriously, how could she? No matter what she was thinking, I couldn't stop. I had to tell her everything.

"It was unbelievable—"

Before I could say another word, Megan interrupted, "Why didn't you take me with you? You know I would love to go flying, and you left me?"

Now I was sure she thought I was spoofing. I wanted so much for her to believe me. Somehow, I had to convince her. I gently grabbed her hands and looked right into her eyes. I tried to be as serious and sincere as I knew how.

"Megan, listen." I took a deep breath and then continued, "Look. I know it sounds crazy, but I'm serious. I'm not kidding. Something happened last night. I went flying in the clouds. I don't know how, but it was so real. I was up above the trees. I was diving and swooping like a bird. It was the most incredible feeling…and it was real. I'm telling you, Megan. I was up there." I pointed out the window again. Now I could tell I had her attention. I actually thought she believed me or wanted to. At least I could tell she knew that this wasn't a prank.

"Billy, you're serious, aren't you? I mean you really think, I mean you really did go flying last night? How is that possible? How did it happen?"

"I don't know. The whole thing still doesn't make sense to me, but I know what I felt."

I definitely had her attention, but I could tell she was still thinking. She was still trying to figure me out. "Billy, I believe you. I do. I don't think you're making this up, but think about it. It's impossible. I mean how could that really happen? Maybe it was a dream… That's it. It had to be dream. They can be very real, you know."

"I thought that too, Megan. That's the first thing I thought of when I woke up this morning, but it was so real. I don't know. I honestly don't know." After a pause I added, "And what's so weird is that I don't feel tired. I mean, how could I be up all night and still feel like I've had the best sleep ever? I just don't get it."

"Well, isn't that your answer?" Megan said. "It had to be a dream. You must have been asleep. After all, I've never been flying, but it's got to be tiring, especially if you're new at it!" Her little jab helped me relax a little.

"Well, I guess, I'm just a natural, that's why I don't feel tired. I must have the gift!" I declared with a big grin. We both laughed a little at that.

I was thinking to myself, *Well, so far, so good. I just told her that I went flying, and she's still listening.* I paused for a moment and took a deep breath. I was really nervous about the next part. How could I then tell her that I actually met and talked with the cloud people? I also knew that there was no way I could stop now. I had to tell her everything. I had to tell someone, and she was the best person I knew to share my secret with.

"Okay, Megan. I haven't told you everything yet. I mean flying and all was cool, but there was even more." I stopped for a moment to get enough courage to continue. "It wasn't just that I was flying, but…" I waited for a little longer before I said the next words, but then they finally came out. "I actually met them. Yes, I met the cloud people…and I talked to them."

I stopped for a moment to try to see how she took it. I couldn't tell what was going through her mind. She just had this big blank look on her face. I decided that I just better keep going, so I continued. "Their leader, or at least the one who did the talking, was Zon. He's really nice. He's married and everything. Well, they don't call it husband and wife, but it's kind of the same."

Once I started, I couldn't stop. I don't how long I was talking, but I just kept going. Megan didn't say anything as she sat in her bed. She just stared at me and let me keep going and going and going. I told her everything that happened. As I continued talking, I could see the look on her face changed. I could tell she was starting to get into it. I couldn't tell if it was because she believed me or just that she caught up in what I was saying. Finally, after rattling on and on, I stopped long enough for her to speak.

"So you're telling me that you were right in front of these cloud guys? I mean right in front of them?" I just nodded my head." "Right there? What was that like? I mean do they really have bodies? How did you talk with them? What do their voices sound like?"

As much as I had rambled on, it was now her turn. She started firing questions at me. As much as I thought I had told her, she obviously still had a lot of questions. I couldn't blame her. If I was in her place, I would have had a lot of questions. As she asked, and I answered, the more I realized how incredible the whole thing was.

After one final question, she put her hands on my shoulders and looked me right in the eye. "Billy, I believe you. I don't think you're trying to pull one over on me, but"—then she paused—"you've got to tell me straight up. Was it real? Are you kidding me? The truth now."

"Megan, I know I'm always clowning around and trying to make a joke, but I'm telling you the truth. This was real. I was up there, and I met them. I don't know how, but it was real!"

Before I could say another word, she gave me a hug. "I believe you, Billy. I believe you." I was so glad that she felt that way. I wanted so much to have someone believe me, and I especially wanted her to believe me.

We were so caught up in the whole thing that neither of us knew what time it was. We then heard Grandma calling up the stairs, "Hey, you two. Aren't you ever going to get up? Breakfast is ready!"

When Grandma called, I knew it was time to get downstairs. Everyone knew not to keep her waiting; besides, I suddenly realized how hungry I was. I guess flying gives you an appetite!

As we walked out of her room, I grabbed Megan's arm. "Believe it or not, I've got more to tell you. We'll finish this later after we eat!"

"Well, I want to hear more. I still have some questions, and I want to know everything. By the way, are you going to say anything at breakfast?"

Before I answered, I ran back into my room to get my slippers. As I walked into my room, I stopped dead in my tracks. A chill went up my spine. Megan had followed me and saw the look on my face.

"Now what's the matter? What's wrong?"

"The window," I said. "My window. It's wide open. I know it was shut last night. I don't like an open window. I remember closing it and locking it last night. Yea, I know it was closed."

"So," said Megan, "what's the big deal? You must have opened it this morning when you got up."

"No, I didn't. The first thing I did was go to your room."

"Well, okay. But I still don't get it. What's the point?"

"What's the point?" I asked. I pointed to the window. "How did it get open? Didn't you hear what I was saying before? Now I can picture it. I distinctly remember going out the window. That's how it started. I went out the window."

"Maybe," she said, then after a pause, "Wait a minute!" She slapped me on the arm. "I was really believing you. Now I know you're up to one of your tricks! You made that whole thing up. You opened the window so it would look like it was real. Come on, Billy. Seriously, flying with the clouds. To think I was believing you. Come on. Flying? No way. You opened the window."

"Honest, Megan. I'm not making it up. You have to—"

Before I could finish, Grandma called upstairs again. "Breakfast is ready!"

"Listen, we better get downstairs. We'll finish this later...but I'm not making it up!"

"Okay," she said. "I'm hungry anyway...but you are making it up!" With that, she pushed me away with an odd look on her face and went charging down the stairs. "I'll race you."

She beat me, as she usually did, and as we ran into the dining room, we discovered that everyone else was already up and eating. Grandma had made bacon and eggs, and the smell was great. Grandpa was already on his second cup of coffee.

Uncle Frank was the first to greet us with his usual sarcasm. "Glad you two could join us for lunch!"

"Ha, ha," I said and then sat down and filled my plate. I love bacon and eggs, especially at Grandma's.

Megan sat next to me and also filled her plate. But she took me by surprise when after her first mouthful, she announced, "Billy has a good reason for being late." She shot me a sarcastic smile. "He had a long night. It seems he spent all night flying." She ended her surprise announcement with a big, dramatic laugh and looked at me as if to say, *There, I got you. Now what are you going to say.*

I couldn't believe she brought it up. I wasn't prepared for that. Before I could collect my thoughts, she continued, "Go ahead, Billy. Tell everyone about your night!"

Her face had a look of triumph as she probably figured she won this time. She certainly succeeded in putting me on the spot. Everyone had stopped eating and was looking at me. I was frantically trying to figure out what to say. I really wished I could have just enjoyed my breakfast. I was hungry, and the bacon and eggs hit the spot, but everyone was looking at me. I knew I had to say something.

Uncle Frank, who could never let something like this go, gave me a short reprieve as he spoke before I could think of a way to begin. "Okay, Billy. Let's hear it. What happened last night? Flying. Wow. Tell us all about it. This, I've got to hear!"

I put another bit of my eggs in my mouth and thought to myself, *Here it goes.* "Listen. Don't laugh. Just give me a chance to tell the whole story. I find it hard to believe myself, but I know it was real." Before I could continue, it suddenly occurred to me. What about the window? I wondered if anyone had opened my window. "Hey, wait a minute. Did anybody go in my room last night and open my window?"

Grandma answered immediately. "Billy, you know you've told me many times that you don't like a draft. I would never open your window. It certainly wasn't me."

Grandpa looked up from his plate at me. "Why do you ask, Billy? What's so important about the window?"

Before I could answer, Uncle Frank, in his typical Uncle Frank way, had to jump in. "Well, it wasn't me, but I did see a UFO in the area last night. Maybe an alien came into your room!"

"Really, Uncle Frank. That's the best you can do? No one talks about UFOs anymore! Seriously, so no one opened my window last night?"

By now, they were all giving me a strange look. Obviously, they couldn't figure out where I was going with this whole thing, but at least I learned that none of them had opened my window. I could tell Uncle Frank was ready with another of his comments, but thankfully, Grandpa beat him to it.

"All right, Billy. Let's have it. What's this all about? What happened last night?"

They were giving me their full attention, waiting for my answer. Before I could figure out some way to slowly lead into my experience, I finally decided to just blurt it out. "I went flying last night. Megan thinks it was a dream, but I was flying. I soared above the house and the whole neighborhood." I paused to take a breath and then kept going. I couldn't turn back now. "And I saw them. I saw the cloud people. They talked to me. Well, they didn't exactly talk. They talk by thinking thoughts and sending them to you."

Uncle Frank let out a huge laugh. "Wow! You've got me beat, kid! That's better than anything I could come up with."

I could see Megan looking around to check everyone's reaction. Grandma just looked down, holding her head in her hands. I could see her slowly shaking her head back and forth. Grandpa had a look that told me he realized that I was serious.

"I've seen and heard a lot of things in my day, but that's one of the most incredible things anyone ever said. I don't know why, but I believe you, Billy. I believe you're convinced this happened. I believe you think you're telling the truth." He paused for a moment and then continued, saying what I'm sure they were all thinking, "But, Billy, flying? I mean *really* flying? Are you sure that you weren't just so caught up with all this talk about the cloud people that you dreamed about it all last night? I mean I've had some pretty real dreams too, but they were just dreams. How is it possible? How did you fly?"

Uncle Frank chimed in, "Yea, Billy. I would love to have been there, but your Grandpa and I had to use jets or helicopters!"

At least that made me smile, but I wasn't changing my story. How could I possibly convince them? "I know it sounds crazy. When I think about it, I find it hard to believe myself, but I know what I felt. Besides, what about the window?"

"I have to admit that's one thing that puzzles me," Megan added.

That comment started what would be the longest breakfast I could ever recall. We discussed my experience from every possible angle. I was glad that as the conversation continued, rather than doubting me, they were genuinely trying to understand exactly what happened and what it all meant. Eventually, the search for a theory turned to questions about the cloud people. Grandpa was especially interested. Even Uncle Frank softened up and sincerely started asking questions. Grandma and Megan sort of sat back and let the two of them lead in the investigation. I still couldn't tell if they believed it

48

actually happened or if they just believed me. One thing was for sure; they were all fascinated by my description of the cloud people.

"So you actually talked to them?" Uncle Frank asked. From his question I could tell he was really thinking. This was a different side to my usually wisecracking uncle.

Before I could answer him, Grandpa jumped in. "Well, remember, Frank, they don't really talk. They kind of send their thoughts. I never spoke to them, but when I encountered them, it did seem to me at the time that somehow they knew what I was thinking."

Before anyone else could continue, Grandma interrupted the discussion. "I hate to put an end to this breakfast, but it's past time for lunch. We were going to the park today, but I guess it's too late for that. Besides, there's no sense in making a lunch if you just had breakfast!"

"I guess not," Grandpa replied. Then after thinking, he added, "Well, I may not be hungry, but I love the park. I'd still like to go. We don't have to eat. It's a beautiful day. Who knows? Maybe we'll see some clouds!"

All I had to hear was the word clouds, and I got really excited. I never liked clearing the table at home, but now I didn't mind!

"That's right, Grandpa. Clouds. Let's go."

I don't think any table had ever been cleared so fast as that day. Everything was brought to the kitchen and put in the dishwasher in no time. With that done, I ran upstairs to get changed. I realized I had been in my pajamas all morning. I was excited at the idea of seeing clouds, but I think I also enjoyed the invitation from Grandpa. The fact that he brought it up made me think that he really believed me. I couldn't wait to get to the park. There just had to be clouds for us to see.

I ran into my room and was about to get changed when I remembered my manners. I could hear Mom's voice in my head reminding me. I stuck my head down the stairs and called out, "Oh, by the way, Grandma. Thanks for breakfast. It was great."

Satisfied that I had done the polite thing, I ran back into my room and got changed. In a flash, I opened the door and was running down the stairs.

"Hey, do you still have those big binoculars? They would be great. Where are they? Do we have them?"

With a chuckle, Grandpa answered from the kitchen, still sipping his coffee, "Okay. Relax. We still have them. I think they're in the cabinet at the end of the hallway. I'll get them."

"Never mind, Grandpa. I'll look!" I ran back upstairs and pulled open the doors on the top of the cabinet, and sure enough, there they were. Great. This was going to be so cool today. I turned to go back downstairs, and without looking, I bumped into Megan and almost knocked her down. "Oh sorry. I didn't see you. Are you okay?"

"Yea, I'm fine. And relax. The park will still be there…and your precious new friends!" As she said that, she gave me a little push and a teasing little smile.

"Well, I know you're gonna like them too," I said. "Just wait and see. They'll be your friends too. Now come on. Let's go."

As I got downstairs, I saw Grandpa still sipping his coffee. I couldn't believe it. "Come on, Grandpa. Please, let's go. We've got some cloud hunting to do!"

With that, he took his last sip and stood up. With a big grin, he told me, "Well, that was my fourth cup of coffee, so I guess I should go. I'll be right there, Billy. Don't worry. I'm sure your friends will wait."

Grandpa was putting his cup in the sink as I ran out the door. I jumped off the porch and dashed to the car. I couldn't wait to get to the park. Before I got in, I turned and saw Megan right behind me. I was surprised that not too far behind her was Grandpa. Back by the door and on the porch was Uncle Frank. He leaned back inside and called out to Grandma. "Are you coming?"

From inside, I heard her respond, "That's okay. All of you go. I still have things to do." Then she poked her head out the door, putting her hand on Uncle Frank's shoulder as she looked out at us. "Don't forget to get some pictures!"

I wasn't sure if she meant it or if she was trying to be funny. I know she didn't mean it, but bringing up pictures only reminded me that I had forgotten my camera. I still couldn't believe I had done that. I sure wished I had it now. "Sure thing, Grandma." With that,

I jumped into the back seat of the car and yelled out the open door, "Now let's go!"

As Uncle Frank jumped in the front passenger seat next to Grandpa who was driving, I kept looking out the window up at the sky. I was hoping for more clouds, but at least there were some. There were just enough to give me hope that Zon and company were up there waiting. Usually in summer, I liked it to be a nice clear-blue sky, but now all I wanted to see were clouds! The more, the better. Well, at least we were finally pulling out the driveway.

Visit to the Park

When we got to the park, I was glad to see that there weren't too many people. There were only a few cars in the parking lot. I only saw one couple walking and then one family by the playground set. It was as if we had the whole park practically all to ourselves. I opened the car door, grabbed Megan's arm, pulling her out behind me.

"Isn't this cool? I just know we're going to see them. You're gonna love them, just like I told you."

As I pulled her out the door, she pulled her hand away, "Okay. Okay. Look, I'm as anxious as you, but I'd like to keep my arm please!"

"Oops, sorry," I told her. I didn't realize how hard I was pulling. I just couldn't help myself, and I really wanted her to see some clouds.

Megan and I had been to that park many times. We even had a favorite tree, perfect for climbing. We spent many hours in it crawling through the branches and lots of time just sitting and talking. With binoculars in hand, I looked at Megan.

"Let's go!"

Before I could move, Megan gave her look and said, "I'll race you!"

With that, she took off like a flash (she always was faster than me), and I started running as fast as I could. I gave it my best, but when I reached the tree, she was already climbing up.

"She beat you again, Billy," Uncle Frank called out as he and Grandpa finally got out of the car.

I found my favorite spot and got settled in. I called down to Uncle Frank, "I know. I know. But I bet I'll find my cloud people first!"

With that, I lifted my binoculars and began scanning the sky. As I did so, Megan, slapped me on the arm. "Hey, what am I looking for? How will I know if I see one?"

"Just a minute. Just a minute. There's a big clump of clouds over there. I just know they're in there. Give me a minute." I zoomed in with the binoculars, and for a second, I thought I saw him. "Wow! Wow! Oh, wait a minute. No. It's not him. I thought I saw him. Darn. I thought it was him."

I took the binoculars away from eyes and looked down for a moment. I was disappointed. They just had to be there. I've got to see them. I wanted to spot them because I wanted to see them, but I think I also wanted to prove to myself and, well, yes, everyone else, that last night was real.

I was so focused on searching the sky that I wasn't paying attention to Megan. I hadn't noticed that she was getting impatient. Finally, she couldn't take it any longer. "Okay, Billy. It's my turn. Let me look. Let me have the binoculars." She kept tapping me on the shoulder. "Come on. Let me see."

I realized that I should let her have a turn, even though I wanted to keep looking. I was so sure that I would see one. Even though they were now pretty far away, that clump of clouds looked perfect for a sighting. As I slowly handed the binoculars to Megan, she almost ripped them out of my hands. "Thanks. Okay. Let's see if I can find one of these things!"

"Good luck." I'm not sure if I meant it. Sure, I wanted her to see them, but the competitor in me still wanted to be first.

Megan began a systematic search of the sky, hoping that she might discover one of the mysterious people. She had no luck, but as she scanned the sky, I suddenly heard her let out a big, "Amazing!"

I jumped right next to her in the tree. My heart was pounding. I started tapping her on the shoulder like a woodpecker. "Well, well, what is it? What do you see? Did you see one?"

She was so caught with what she was looking at, I don't think she even heard me. I persisted. What was she looking at? Finally, after poking her arm and calling her name, she responded, "What? What do you want?"

"What did you see? What's up there? You said, 'Amazing.'"

"Oh, sorry," she replied. "I didn't see any cloud people. I was just noticing how cool the clouds are. I never really paid that much attention to them before. You can actually see all kinds of stuff in them. They're really cool."

"I don't believe you. You got me all excited. I thought you saw one." I did remember all those times I looked up at the sky and was fascinated by the clouds, but that was all in the past. Now that I met the cloud people, that's all I was interested in. Sure, clouds by themselves are cool, but that's nothing compared to Zon and company. "Oh, well, keep on looking. They have to be up there. I can feel it."

We took turns with the binoculars but with no success. We were up in that tree for almost two hours but didn't see anything. I didn't want to give up, but I had to admit that today was not the day. Megan must have heard my thoughts. She gave a look of sympathy like she knew. She patted me on the shoulder. At another time, she would have been busting my chops, but she seemed genuinely concerned.

"Sorry. I was hoping too."

"Well, my vacation isn't over. In fact, it's just begun. There will be more chances. We're gonna find them. I know we will."

As we began climbing down, Grandpa was calling out to us.

"Billy, Megan. Let's go. We have some iced tea."

It was a hot day, and the idea of some of Grandma's homemade cold iced tea sounded really good. We jumped to the ground and ran to the table where Grandpa and Uncle Frank were already sipping their tea.

"Well, kids," said Grandpa, "any luck? You were up there for quite a while."

Megan answered first, "No. We didn't see any cloud people, but you know what? Clouds are pretty cool. It was neat just looking at them. I could sit and look at them for hours. It's kind of like sitting by a campfire. It's so peaceful. It just makes you happy."

While I was happy that she enjoyed clouds just for being clouds, I couldn't hold back my disappointment. "Yea, yea, yea. Clouds are great, Megan, but I want to see my cloud people." I finished gulping down my tea. "Well, at least the iced tea is good. Thank you,

Grandma," I said as I raised my glass in her honor, even though she wasn't with us. Then I looked over at Uncle Frank. "Hey, Uncle Frank. You want to go with me and try another spot? Maybe we'll have better luck."

Megan looked up from her iced tea and only smiled. "Maybe you will have better luck, Uncle Frank. Maybe you should go with him."

"Not so fast," chimed in Grandpa. "Billy, come here a minute. I want to talk to you." His voice and look seemed serious, making me wonder what was on his mind. "You can go look for cloud people, but I just want to show you something first."

I walked over to him, and Grandpa put his hand on my shoulder. He gently walked me a short distance away from the others as if whatever he wanted to say, he didn't want them to hear, only me. With his hand still on my shoulder, he said to me, "Billy, look up at that sky. Isn't it beautiful? God has given us a great world, and there are so many things we still haven't learned about it. I hope you never stop looking and never stop trying to discover new things. But while your head is up in the clouds"—and with that he picked up my right foot and tapped it gently with his other hand—"your feet are on the ground. That's where you have to live, Billy. It's okay to look at the clouds now and then, but if you don't keep your feet on the ground, you're going to miss out on life. Look around you right here. You have family that loves you, a good friend, a vacation, and a beautiful park on a beautiful day. Don't miss life, Billy. When I came back from the war, at first, all I could think about was those cloud people. But you know what? I got so caught up in them I almost missed what was right before me, like your Grandma, the best thing that ever happened to me. I was fortunate that someone talked some sense into me before it was too late. They told me what I'm telling you now. Keep your feet on the ground. Don't let life pass you by. Remember, keep your feet on the ground!"

I was quiet for a minute, absorbing what Grandpa had said. I had great respect for him and wanted to learn from him, but I was also still so excited about this new quest. "Grandpa, I know what you're saying, but it's so hard. How can I do that? I can't stop thinking about the cloud people, and after last night, I just know I have to see them. I feel like it's my mission or something. I could be the one to make a great discovery."

"I never said it was easy," replied Grandpa, "but you can do it. In fact, who said you can't do both. What it takes is discipline. You can make yourself do stuff you might not otherwise do. No, it's not easy, but it can be done." With that he gave me a pat on the head, a big hug, and then looked me in the eye. "You'll figure it out... Just don't forget us when you become famous for your discovery!"

Grandpa always had a lot of wisdom, and I tried my best to hold on to what he was telling me. I knew he was right, but it was so tough. "Okay, Grandpa. I'll try. Thanks." Then after a pause, I said, "Now can I go find another tree and look some more?"

Grandpa just shook his head and laughed. I think he knew what I was going through. After all, he was young once! "Sure, Billy. Go ahead...and good luck!"

It was a great day in the park, but there were no sightings of cloud people. Uncle Frank even climbed another tree with me and took his turn with the binoculars. I think he was really trying to find them too. After a little while, he got tired of the search and climbed down.

"Hey, Megan. Your turn, again."

She must have been waiting because before I knew it, she was right up there next to me, ready for a turn with the binoculars. I'm not sure when it happened, but after a few turns with the binoculars, Megan and I ended up just sitting there talking. After a bit, we started using the binoculars to check out the other people in the park. More people had come while we were busy cloud searching. We began looking at them and making up stories about who they were and what they were like. It was fun.

Then I heard a voice from below. "Hey, guys. It's time to go. We'd better get going. Grandpa's getting sleepy, and remember, he's driving! Besides, I'm sure Grandma's starting to wonder where we are."

I really didn't want to go. It was still nice out, and Megan and I were having such a good time. I still can't believe that we had that much fun without any cloud people sightings. Yes, it was a good day, but I had to admit it was time to leave. When we got to car, before I got in, I went over to Grandpa.

"Wait a minute, Grandpa." He stopped and looked back at me. I reached up and put my hand on his shoulder then, with the other, hit my foot with the other hand. "Thanks, Grandpa. It was a great day."

He didn't say anything. With his usual smile, he gave me a pat on the head.

A Quiet Evening

By now, it was late afternoon. As Grandpa pulled into the driveway, he looked at us and put his finger to his lips. "Let's be quiet. This is Grandma's nap time." Then after a pause and a wink, he said, "And I won't be far behind. It was very tiring watching you climb those trees!"

We very quickly emptied the car and tiptoed up the steps. I never noticed before, but that door sure did creak, as much as we tried to do it slowly. We managed to get inside without too much noise. Grandpa excused himself, and then Uncle Frank said, "And I have to make some phone calls."

I was a little tired but certainly not ready for a nap. I looked at Megan and asked, "So what shall we do?"

"I don't know. What do you want to do?" I didn't have to give it too much thought. My grandparents had some cool books in the den. The last time I visited, I had started looking at a book on war planes that Grandpa had. I thought this would be a good time to get back into it. "Well, if you don't have anything in mind, I was thinking of getting my grandfather's book on war planes and looking at that."

Megan was a great student, and she loved to read. She also knew the books in the den. "Okay. That sounds good. I'll check out their books too."

I grabbed my book and quietly walked upstairs to my room. Megan went in to make her selection. Within a very short time, the house was quiet with sleeping and reading.

I quickly dove into my grandfather's book. Especially after hearing his story I was anxious to study more about airplanes. I was hoping that I could find some information about the kind of jet he flew and was even curious about those Russian Migs. However, after about a half hour of reading in my room, I decided to go out on the porch. There was that great rocking chair, and it was so nice outside. I always preferred to be outside any chance I got, particularly in the summer. So I quietly went downstairs to go out on the porch. First, I had to negotiate the squeaky door, and just as I was closing it behind me, there was Megan.

"I'll join you," she said. I grabbed the treasured rocking chair, leaving Megan to sit on one of the others.

Looking back, I probably shouldn't have gone outside, even though it was a nice day. I had no sooner sat down to read when I couldn't resist any longer. The fighter jets were interesting and all, but there was the sky…right up there…calling out to me. I couldn't resist. I put the book down and walked off the porch and looked up at the sky. As I gazed upward, I suddenly felt someone next to me—Megan. It didn't take much to distract her from her book. I didn't say anything, and we both just stood there, staring at the sky. Without warning, Megan took a step back and gave me a light punch on the arm.

"What was that all about?" I asked.

"Why can't I see them? I mean I'm jealous. I'm starting to think that your cloud people don't like women! After all, Grandma and I are the only ones here who haven't seen them—and we're girls!" As I was trying to think of a comeback, she put her face right in mine. "I want to see them. What do *your* friends have against us women?"

"You're crazy," I said. "It's got nothing to do with being a boy or girl. It's just that they only choose *special* people." I added that emphasis with the biggest grin. As soon as the words came out of my mouth, something inside of me said I better start running. Sure enough, as soon as I took off, Megan was right behind, and her face told me she meant business. Unfortunately, she was faster and caught up with me in a flash. I was lucky that she didn't reach me until I got to a soft part of the yard because she tackled me as good as any defensive back. In a split second, she was on top of me, and I was ready to cover my face when she gave me a big grin.

"Maybe it's not a boy-girl thing. Maybe it's just that they can't see that well, or they're not a very good judge of character!" For emphasis, she gave me a light slap on the face.

Before I could come up with a response, Grandma came out on the porch and called out, "Is anybody hungry?"

For a moment, I wasn't sure if dinner really was ready, or if she was just trying to save me! Anyway, looking for clouds all day, we had barely eaten. All Megan and I had were some chips with our iced tea. Not only did Grandma save me from Megan, she also heard the cry of my stomach. Thanks, Grandma!

Funny how food will bring an instant truce. We both jumped up and ran to the porch. Megan beat me again, but I really didn't care. I was hungry.

"Wash your hands. I saw you wrestling on the ground," Grandma reminded us.

Grandpa just smiled. In a jiff, we were at the table, and there was a big plate of leftover fried chicken with a pile of baked potatoes next to it and a bowl of salad.

"Hey, where's Uncle Frank?" I asked.

Just as I said that, he walked into the room. "Sorry, I was making some phone calls. I have a surprise for you."

"What? What?"

Before he could answer, Grandma interrupted, "It will have to wait. You know, Billy, grace comes first."

"Oh, yes. That's right."

As soon as Grandpa finished the prayer, Megan and I in unison looked at Uncle Frank. "Okay. What's up? What's this big surprise?"

"I'll tell you what. You better grab something to eat first because once I tell you, you're gonna forget about eating."

Now he really had my curiosity, but I was also hungry. So I turned my thoughts from the surprise to some fried chicken.

We were enjoying our food, but I kept looking over at Uncle Frank, waiting for him to talk. He just smiled as he continued eating, managing to throw me a grin in between bites. I even noticed Grandpa and Grandma looking over. I don't think even they knew what was coming.

Finally, Uncle Frank spoke, "Okay. Okay. During dessert."

Megan picked up her napkin and threw it at him, followed by mine. Dinner was good, but I barely tasted it as I waited for the big announcement. At last, the table was cleared, and Grandma brought out some cupcakes and put them down. As soon as she put them down, I blurted out, "Okay, Uncle Frank. Dessert. So what gives? What's this big surprise?"

"Well. Here it is. I have a friend who has a hot air balloon business—"

Before he could continue, I started jumping up and down by my seat. "Yes! Yes! Yes! That will be so cool. Yes! It's a perfect way to get up there and see them. It's going to be great. Oh, wow, this is great!"

Uncle Frank was obviously pleased that he could share the good news, but he had to give me a little dose of reality. "Okay, Billy. Calm down. We're not scheduled till the day before you leave, and it depends on the weather. If there's too much wind or a threat of rain, we won't be able to go, and that's your last night here. So you better start praying the weather's good!"

"I will. Oh, and I'll check the Weather Channel too. It will be great. I just know it."

I jumped up to go turn on the TV, but Grandpa put his hand in the air.

"Just a minute. This is great news, Frank, but before you go anyplace Billy, remember, we finish eating before leaving the table. Chew your food, swallow, and when we're done…and the table is cleared, then you can check."

He gave me a gentle smile, but I knew he was serious. Normally, I would have remembered my grandparents' rule, but I got so excited.

"Sorry, Grandpa. Oops, I forgot."

"It's all right. I understand your excitement. But the weather's not going to change in another twenty minutes. The forecast will still be the same."

Of course, besides being obedient, Grandma's cupcakes were great. Before long, dessert was over, and I rushed to help clear the table. I excused myself and dashed into the sitting room to put on the TV. Megan was right behind me.

"It figures. Commercials! I just want the weather," I yelled at the TV. After the commercials, the weather person started talking about the weather in *other* parts of the country. "I don't care about that right now," I blurted out, causing Megan to laugh.

Finally, after all the delays, they got to the important part, the local forecast. It seemed like it took forever...first, the overnight (that was fine) and then tomorrow, sunny and warm, and finally the important part, the extended forecast. I was almost afraid to look. I still had a few days to wait, but I was hoping for a good stretch of weather leading up to "balloon day." I knew things could change, but the projection looked good. The days were supposed to be sunny and *no* chance of rain—*perfect!*

Megan and I both jumped up off the sofa and started jumping up and down. "Great!" After a moment's celebration, Uncle Frank came into the room.

"Well, what's the forecast? We looking good?" I gave him a two-thumbs-up, and even Uncle Frank couldn't help but give a huge smile. "That's great. I'm really happy for you."

Just then, Grandma walked into the room. "Well, that's good news. I'm glad too. And now I have some more good news. Remember our summer tradition?" I quickly searched my memory to try to recall, and just as I remembered, Grandma made her announcement. "Tonight, it's our annual 'Laurel and Hardy Night' and...homemade ice cream. Grandpa made vanilla and strawberry—that's for you, Megan," she added with a wink.

"A balloon ride for my last night here, homemade ice cream, Laurel and Hardy—it just doesn't get better," I said.

After dinner and clearing the table, I had a little bit of time, so I went upstairs to do some more reading. With clouds on my mind, I really didn't get too far that afternoon. This time, I finally managed to get into my Abraham Lincoln. In fact, I lost track of time.

"Billy. Megan. It's show time," yelled Grandma.

I finished the last two sentences on my page, put in my marker, and joined Megan at the top of steps. I was going to race, but

Grandma was by the bottom of the steps, so better not risk it! We uncharacteristically slowly walked down the stairs.

Grandpa was already in his seat, yes, with his cup of coffee. Uncle Frank pulled up his seat, and Megan, me, and Grandma got the couch. My friends at school always made fun of me for liking Laurel and Hardy, but I thought they were great. I looked forward to this every year. I'm still not sure if it was them or just being with my grandparents, but I loved it. That night's selection was one of my favorites, *The Flying Deuces,* where Laurel and Hardy joined the French Foreign Legion. As usual, we paused in the middle to get our ice cream, another tradition. I loved ice cream, but there was something special about homemade, especially at my grandparents' house.

The movie was over and the ice cream gone when I got distracted. I had been so caught up in the movie that I was surprised that my thoughts quickly changed direction. I started thinking that it was getting closer to bedtime. That meant sleeping, and that meant dreaming. What was going to happen tonight? Would I go flying? It must have showed on my face because Grandma tapped me on my knee.

"Billy. Where are you? What are you thinking?" She didn't miss anything.

"Oh, Grandma. Sorry. I was just thinking about tonight. I was wondering if I was going flying again."

"Well, if you do," Megan chimed in, "be sure and take me. I'd *love* to go flying!"

"Sorry. Remember, the cloud people only invite those that are *special*," I replied and then quickly covered my face for an anticipated slap.

"Well, you'd better leave the window open just in case," Uncle Frank added. "Oh, and just be sure to be back in time for breakfast."

"Ha ha," I said. "Very funny. I'll show you all. I'm going flying tonight. I just know it—"

"Well, I'll tell you what. It's still not too late," interrupted Grandpa. "What do you say? Why don't you get ready for bed, and we'll play a quick game of cards?"

Grandpa loved cards, and it was still early for a summer night. I figured a quick hand would relax me and get me ready for what I hoped was a long night. Megan and I both changed and came back down.

Before I sat down, Grandpa looked at me and said, "Hey, Billy, what happened to your pajamas? They're ripped at the bottom of your one leg."

I stood up to look at my pajama pants, and sure enough, the right leg had a tear. It even looked like some of it was missing. "Gosh, Grandpa. You're right. They are ripped. You know what? I think they've always been like that. I don't remember tearing them. Besides, they're comfortable."

"Boys," Grandma said. "You can't take care of anything. Well, give them to me tomorrow, and I'll fix them. But now, I'm tired. I'm going to bed. Enjoy your cards." Grandma paused before she went to her room, "Oh, and if you go flying, keep it down. Try not to wake me."

"Don't worry. I promise!" I said.

After Grandma left, we had a quick game of rummy. I came close, but Grandpa won again.

"I almost got you, Grandpa. Look out. I'm coming for you next time!"

He just smiled and said, "But you still lost."

"Next time. Next time," I replied. "Well, I should get to bed. After all, I have a long night ahead of me!"

Megan stood up next to me, "And remember, Billy. If you go, you'd better take me or else!"

"Okay, but it's not up to me. It's up to them," I said as I pointed my finger up in the air.

"Well, you kids have a good time, but I'm going to sleep in," Uncle Frank said. "It's very exhausting making phone calls."

We all laughed. As I turned to go upstairs, I noticed that Grandpa had already dozed off in his chair. That caused us to laugh even more, and even though that wasn't our intention, we woke him up.

"What did I miss?" Grandpa asked as he opened his eyes.

"Oh, nothing," Uncle Frank responded. "We're going to bed, and Billy here is going flying!"

"Oh," Grandpa added rather matter-of-factly, offering me no reaction. He quietly got up and turned to us. "Good night."

With him leading the way, each of us followed. Before Megan went to her room, she stopped and gave me a look. She didn't say anything at first. She just looked and then came over and gave me a hug. She whispered in my ear, "Billy. I really do hope you go flying." Then after she stepped back, she punched me on the arm "And you better take me!"

With that, she went into her room and closed the door. I smiled to myself and turned to go into my room. As I walked to the bed, I couldn't help but wonder…what will happen tonight?

Nighttime

Before I got into bed, I just stared at the window. I kept thinking to myself, *Should I leave it open, or should I close it?* I wanted to leave it open just in case I went flying, but then I also thought that if I closed it, and I *did* go flying, that would prove that it was real. Then again, if I went flying, and the window was still closed, that would mean it was only a dream. I don't know how long I stood there, but I just couldn't make up my mind. Finally, I decided to close the window, and for extra proof, I locked my door so that no one could say they came in through the night and opened it. With my mind finally made up, I hopped into bed, but now my heart was pounding in anticipation. I was so keyed up I couldn't settle down. My mind was racing, and I was wide awake.

To make matters worse, I then started thinking that maybe, I should stay awake so I could experience the whole thing. That night of flying was so incredible, and I wanted to do it again. I just had to go flying. I wanted to see the clouds again. As I lay there with my thoughts racing, I couldn't know that all through the house, everyone was also having trouble sleeping. Megan lay wide awake in the room next door. Uncle Frank was sitting in his room looking out the window. Even Grandma and Grandpa were lying in bed, still awake.

Each time I looked at the clock, the hands had only moved a few minutes. The night was barely moving, I was wide awake, and I wasn't flying. I eventually got up and started walking around the room. Finally, maybe out of desperation, and I still can't believe I actually did it, I started flapping my arms. I remember thinking, *Maybe I just have to get started.* Realizing what I was doing, I started laughing to myself. I was literally driving myself crazy. This was getting me nowhere. I should just go back to bed and try to go to sleep. I went back to bed.

"Yea. Right." As soon as my head hit the pillow, there I was, wide awake again. Well, I figured I just wasn't going to get any sleep. I might as well face it. I would be up all night. Then my mind drifted back to last night. I remembered the thrill of flying. As my imagination took me up in the air, my body still lay in the bed. I wasn't going anywhere, but being distracted with those thoughts, I finally drifted peacefully off to sleep. It was 3:00 a.m. Ironically, at that exact time, almost as if on cue, everyone else got out of bed to check on me, Megan, Uncle Frank, Grandpa, and even Grandma. They all met in the hallway, startled to see one another. They each hushed a laugh as the silliness of the scene struck them. They managed to keep their giggles muffled because they didn't want to wake me, that is, if I was in fact asleep in my room.

Finally, Uncle Frank motioned to the others and quietly walked to my room. He tried to open the door only to discover that it was locked. He shrugged his shoulders as he looked at the others to indicate his finding. He gave the handle one more little shake just to be sure. It was locked. Everyone began to wonder what that might mean. As they each considered their own theories, Uncle Frank held up his finger to signal that he had an idea. With that, he walked down the hallway to the stairs. Megan followed. It became clear where he was headed.

They both went downstairs and out the porch door. A little excited at what they might find, they both ran out into the yard underneath my room. They looked up in anticipation, only to discover that my room was dark, and the window closed. Even so, both Uncle Frank and Megan simultaneously then looked up in the sky, just in case I happened to be floating above them. Nothing. Finally admitting that nothing was happening and wasn't going to happen, they went back inside to share their findings with Grandma and Grandpa.

Everyone was a little disappointed but also relieved. They could now all go to sleep. And that's what they did. No one moved until the next morning. Probably because I was the first to fall asleep, I was the first one awake, or so I thought. I propped up my head in bed and glanced over at the window. It was closed. I quickly surveyed the room, not exactly sure what I was looking for, but I didn't see anything out of place. Apparently, I had slept last night and nothing else. No flying and no dreaming. Now I was starting to have some doubts. I didn't see any clouds in the park. I didn't go flying last night. Maybe all this stuff wasn't real. Maybe I just imagined the whole thing. I was so disheartened.

Grandpa's Wisdom

My disappointment though quickly gave way to concern. I realized that everyone, especially Uncle Frank, would give me a good ribbing. For a brief moment, I considered telling a lie and trying to convince everyone that I had gone flying, but I just couldn't. I knew it would be wrong to lie. Both my parents and grandparents had told me that over and over again. Besides, I could never convince them. They would see right through me. They knew me too well. No, I would just have to face the music, but at least, it would be over another great breakfast, courtesy of Grandma.

When I got downstairs, everyone else was already there. From the aroma, I knew that Grandma had made pancakes. I nervously greeted everyone. "Good morning," and then before anyone had a chance to say anything, I quickly added, "and *no*, I didn't go flying. I just slept."

Megan was the first to answer, "I know. We all checked." She covered her mouth and giggled. "In the middle of the night, we all ended up in the hallway by your room. Your door was locked. Uncle Frank and I even went outside to look at your room. The window was closed. We figured if you weren't up in the air by then, you wouldn't have any time, so we all went to bed." Then her expression changed. She even looked a little sad. "Sorry. I was kind of hoping you would fly."

"Well," said Uncle Frank, "remember you have time, and don't forget your last night, hot air balloon!"

"Hey, you're right, Uncle Frank. I almost forgot. I was so worried about flying last night I didn't think of that. In fact, I think I'll check the weather again."

"Not so fast, young man," Grandma interrupted. "Let's eat breakfast first, then you can check your weather." I was disappointed, but managed to soothe my feelings with Grandma's pancakes.

I was so worried about admitting that nothing happened last night, but it turned out to be a great, normal breakfast with good food and good laughs. I even managed to help clean up, at a normal pace, when we were done. But as soon as the last dish hit the sink in the kitchen, I excused myself. Just to be sure, I checked with Grandma. "May I be excused? I mean is it okay to check the weather?"

She looked at me with her soft grin. "Yes, Billy. Go ahead."

With her blessing, I ran into the den to put on the television to check the weather. I don't know what I expected since I just checked it last night, but I couldn't help it. Once again, Megan was right behind me. Before I could get to the Weather Channel, everyone was also in the den, yes, even Grandma. Everyone squeezed on the couch and sat in anticipation of the forecast. Yesterday, the prediction was for a great week. I was hoping, and I'm sure so was everyone else on the couch, for the same. Everyone was so still; for a moment it seemed as if we weren't even breathing. Of course, we had to wait through the commercials, and then finally, what we all were waiting for—the local forecast. It was perfect. The weather was going to be clear, no chance of rain, and no winds! Perfect. Megan and I at the same time jumped up and down. This is going to be great. I couldn't wait.

Then it hit me. I stopped jumping. I slumped back down on the couch with a blank look on my face.

"What's the matter, Billy?" Megan asked.

"It's going to be clear," I said. "Clear. That means no clouds. What if there are no clouds? What's the point of going up in the balloon?"

With that, Megan got the same blank look on her face, and she slumped down on the couch next to me. "You're right. I never thought of that. What are we going to do?"

Uncle Frank stood up and got right in front of both of us. "Hey, guys. Relax. It's going to be *mostly* clear. There should be some clouds. Don't give up. You still may see your friends!"

That was just what I needed to hear. So in the next moment, Megan and I were back up jumping up and down. Grandpa and Grandma just looked at us and laughed, shaking their heads.

It was a beautiful day. It was a perfect day to be on vacation, but time just seemed to drag. I couldn't wait. I don't remember what time it was, but later that day, Grandpa found me sitting on the porch, staring at the sky. He came and sat next to me.

"I think it's time for another little pep talk. Billy, I know you want to be up in that balloon, but you can't just sit here on the porch wasting a beautiful day. Remember the feet?" He picked up my right foot and gave it a tap.

"I know. I know. But it's so hard. I can't help it. I just know we're going to see something. I can feel it."

Grandpa put his hand on my shoulder, just like he did the other day in the park. "Since my foot lecture doesn't seem to have taken, I guess I have to get a little more philosophical with you."

"What do you mean philosophical?" I asked.

"*Agite quod agitis*," he said with a smile.

"What?" I asked.

"*Agite quod agitis*," he said. "It's Latin. It means, 'do what you're doing.' Lots of time, we may want to be doing something else, but we have to stick to what we're doing at the moment. Otherwise, you miss out on life. Right now, you're on vacation. You should be doing vacation stuff and not wasting your time wishing you were doing something else. Believe it or not, I'm excited for that balloon ride. I've waited for a chance like this for over fifty years. But right now, I'm going to finish fixing the shingles on the garage, and then I'm taking a nap. That's *agite quod agitis*."

I just looked at him. Again I knew he was right, but I was a kid, and I wanted to go up in a balloon and find my cloud people. I wanted to enjoy the day, but I just couldn't get my mind off the clouds and the flight.

"I'll tell you what," Grandpa said. "I have a great idea. The grass needs cutting. I hate to do it, so you can take your mind out of the clouds and focus on the lawn mower!"

"So I guess that Latin stuff means get up and get to work?" I said.

"Well, in a way, yes. So how about it? What do you say you cut the lawn? It will help me out and take your mind off things."

"Okay. I'll do it."

"Great." Grandpa got up off the chair. With a smile and a pat on my head, he added, "*Agite quod agitis.*"

So it was off to the garage to get the mower. I had cut the grass before, so I knew the routine. After a few swipes of the grass, I heard the sound of Grandpa nailing some shingles on the garage roof. He looked down at me and nodded his approval. He continued with his shingles, and I kept cutting the grass. I got about one-third of the way done, and I saw Megan on the porch. She was drinking iced tea, but I could tell that she was deliberately trying to tease me. She dramatically took a big swallow, licked her lips, and gave me a big smile. I took the bait. I shut the mower off and ran up onto the porch.

"That wasn't nice. It's hot in the sun."

"Too bad," she added. Then she reached next to her to present another glass of iced tea. "Here you go. I figured you needed a break." Then she mumbled but loud enough for me to hear, "Even though you only did a few rows!"

Before I could answer, Grandpa was at the door. How did he get done so quickly? "Okay, Billy. Enjoy your iced tea and then finish. Remember." With that he looked at Megan and winked. I knew what was coming. They both looked at me and, together, said, "*Agite quod agitis!*" Obviously, Grandpa had prepped her. She just looked at me with a smile and lifted her glass before taking another sip.

By the time I finished (they had a pretty big yard), it was late afternoon. I was hot and tired. As I walked in the door, Grandma was in the kitchen.

"Good job. Why don't you grab a quick shower and cool off? We're going to barbecue tonight, so you have enough time."

That sounded great. The shower felt so good, and by the time I was dried off and changed, I felt refreshed and ready for the evening. When I came downstairs, Megan greeted me. I was surprised to see that she was wearing a bright summer dress.

"Well. I didn't know tonight was formal," I said as I looked at her.

With that, she twirled around and asked, "Do you like it?'"

"Well, I guess. Yea, it's nice." I think that was the first time I saw her in a dress.

Just then, Uncle Frank walked in and said, "Yes. If I had known, I would have worn a tie."

That would have been unusual. I know I had never seen Megan in a dress, but I also knew I *never* saw Uncle Frank in a tie.

"Well, it doesn't matter," Grandpa added. "No matter how you're dressed, you're getting hamburgers. How do you guys want them cooked?"

It was a perfect evening, and I loved the smell of hamburgers cooking on the grill. As we waited for them to be done, we had some salad and more iced tea. I don't know how, but somehow, I managed to forget the clouds and enjoy a great evening in the backyard.

After dinner, Grandma looked at Megan and me and said, "Why don't you two take a walk. There's still some light. In a while, we'll have s'mores for you both to enjoy."

With that, we looked at each other and slowly got up. "Okay." I said to Megan, "Let's go."

I guess it was the dress, but that night I started to look at Megan a little differently than I was used to. That evening, she wasn't just the girl I raced and teased. I'm not sure how long we were walking and talking. We had a nice chat about a lot of things but, of course, ended up in the clouds.

Just as we began talking about my favorite topic, Grandma called out. "It's time. We have all the fixings. Come on and enjoy."

By then it was pretty dark but a perfect night for a fire and s'mores. It was a great end to a very nice day and evening. With that fire and cooking marshmallows and talking and laughing, I managed to get through the day. I was still thinking about clouds and the balloon ride, but I did manage a little bit of Grandpa's *agite*.

It was time to get ready for bed. I looked at Grandpa. "Thanks," I said, and he just winked at me. Then I looked at Megan. "I had a good time tonight."

Megan then surprised me. She leaned over and gave me a quick little kiss on the cheek. "I had a good time too," she said with a nervous giggle and ran to go upstairs.

I just stopped and looked at Grandpa, Grandma, and Uncle Frank.

"Okay, Casanova," he said, "time for bed. Tomorrow's another day."

As he turned to walk away, I asked, "What's Casanova?"

He just laughed. "Never mind. Get some sleep." With that, I turned my attention to thoughts of clouds, flying and, soon, a balloon ride. I couldn't wait.

Before everyone left for bed, Grandpa stood up and motioned for attention. "Before we go to bed, I have an announcement to make. Don't misunderstand me, Billy, but I'm tired. I hope you go flying or have a great dream or whatever, but I'm tired. I'm going to bed, and I'm going to sleep. If you go out the window, you're on your own. Have a great flight, and I'll see you in the morning!"

Grandma followed suit and simply added, "Me too! Goodnight." With that they both went into their room and closed the door.

Megan had come back downstairs, and she and Uncle Frank were left standing with me in the sitting room.

"I'm not so sure myself," said Uncle Frank. "I just might get up again to check in on you. How about it, Megan? Do you think you'll be awake too?"

"Wait a minute. How can you be so sure I won't go out the window too," Megan said with a bit of indignation. "I just might go flying myself. Who knows? Maybe those cloud people will like me better." She turned to look at me with a smug grin on her face, slightly sticking out her tongue for emphasis.

Of course, I couldn't let it go, so I immediately responded, "Not possible, Megan. You see, they already told me that they liked me and to tell you not to bother."

The last words had barely slipped out my tongue, and Megan reached out for me. I dashed out the door on to the porch. Even in her dress, she was faster than me. As soon as she caught up with me, she gave me a few slaps on the arm.

"I can't believe I said I had a good time tonight! You're unbelievable."

Of course, she was laughing as she said that. Before I could say anything, Uncle Frank poked his head out the door with his finger over his lips. "Heh, guys. Keep it down. Remember your grandparents? Remember sleep?"

Almost on cue, I heard Grandpa's door open. "Quiet please." That's all he had to say.

The night was over, and it was time to actually go to bed. I looked at Megan and offered a smile in truce. She returned the look. With that, we came back inside and upstairs to our rooms. With a whisper, we each said, "Good night," and went into our rooms. At last the house was quiet, but things were just about to happen...

A Thrilling Night

As pumped up as I was in anticipation, surprisingly, I fell almost immediately to sleep. Next door, just as amazing, Megan also managed to quickly drift off to sleep. However, her sleep did not last for long. In a little more than an hour, Megan was wide awake. There was only one thing wrong. When she opened her eyes, she was not in her bed! It happened! She was in the air above the house. At first, she panicked, and almost by instinct, she began to flap her arms just as I had done, thinking that would prevent her from falling. To her surprise, she realized that she wasn't going to fall. No, she was flying!

Gradually, what was happening began to sink in. She kept saying to herself, *Megan, you're flying. You're actually flying!* After a few more moments, she was able to add, *This is cool. This is really cool! If only Billy could see me now!* She was filled with so much excitement and filled with so much energy that suddenly, she took off like a rocket into the sky. Normally, that would have terrified her, but strangely, she felt no fear. She was instantaneously comfortable with flying. She was a natural. It felt as if she had done this all of her life. Without hesitation, she flew up in a vertical path, then turning to dive toward the ground, swooping upward at the last minute. She repeated this motion many times with great delight. After mastering the dive, she turned her attention to loop the loops. Not even a veteran pilot could have matched her precision and speed.

Megan was completely caught up in the thrill of flying when she was suddenly distracted by a voice. It came from somewhere down below, but she couldn't pinpoint it. She heard it again. She stopped flying and stood motionless in midair as she searched the ground. She was actually so high up that she could barely make out anything on the ground. She slowly descended, scanning the area below her to see if she could see anybody. Then she was startled to hear the voice just off to her right. It sounded as if it was only a few feet away. She turned, and to her surprise, there I was! I don't know how long she was up there, but I had been floating around for almost a half hour before I noticed her. I was amazed at how quickly she learned.

Then for a moment I thought. Gosh. *She's not only faster than me on the ground, but now she can fly better.* Still, I was really glad to see her. Not only would I have her company, but she could be a witness.

"Hey, I see you made it! Not bad. I was watching you, but I think I'm better," I said, even though I knew I wasn't. "After all, Megan, you're just a beginner!" With those words, our race in the air was on. "Bye." I took off like a race car, only glancing back to see where she was.

No sooner had I looked back than I saw Megan not only catching up to me but swooshing past me. I felt her wind, and indeed, she was as fast in the air as she was on the ground. She effortlessly got past me and was just far enough in front of me. She stopped in mid-air and, as if lying on the floor, propped up her head with her hands and coyly said as I approached, "Hi. Where have you been?"

I couldn't let it go, so I reached out to grab her to hold her back, but before my hands could even get close, she was gone in a flash. With that, our aerial chase began. We were like two bees, darting back and forth across the sky. If we were on the ground, we would have looked like two squirrels chasing one another through the branches of a tree.

After a while, we finally stopped chasing each other. We weren't really tired but just wanted a break. As we paused in the air, the expression on Megan's face suddenly changed.

"Do you hear that?" she asked.

I listened and realized I heard it too. I started getting excited. Could it be? My eyes turned away from Megan and looked around. Sure enough, we were not alone! I looked back at Megan, hardly able to contain myself.

"Look around you," I quietly whispered.

She then turned her head to look around, and her mouth popped open. All around us were countless faces. We were surrounded by cloud people! It was almost as if we were in a stadium, and the cloud people were in the stands watching us. After the initial joy of seeing them, I then quickly turned my attention to try and locate my friend. I began to systematically survey the faces to find Zon but with no luck. I didn't see him. Indeed, I had to be honest with myself. They all did look alike!

As I continued looking at all the cloud faces, I then noticed the expression on Megan's face. She was just staring in silence. As I slowly floated back away from her, she started yelling: "They're real! They're real! They're real! I can see them. They're real! They're real!"

"Okay, Megan. Yes, they're real. Calm down. Get a hold of yourself!"

I have to admit that I was a bit annoyed but, actually, more embarrassed at her outburst. I nervously looked around to see the reaction of the cloud people. They were all smiling. In fact, they were all laughing so "loud" that the air around them seemed to shake. As Megan calmed down, she noticed the laughter around her. Like all laughter, it was infectious, and in the next moment, she was laughing with them. I was relieved at their reaction, glad that they weren't offended at Megan's enthusiasm.

As the laughter gradually faded, Megan began to realize what I discovered my first time meeting the cloud people. I could tell what she was thinking. She was realizing that even though they were laughing, she couldn't hear anything. I could sense the questions running through her head. *Billy, what's going on? I can hear them, but I can't hear them. The sound is in my head. I don't understand.*

I smiled and began to explain, except that, almost by instinct, I didn't talk to her with my voice. I was only sending my thoughts to her. I was speaking to her in the head, just the way I learned on the first night. I still don't know how I did, but it came so naturally to me. I was trying to get her to understand. *Remember what I was saying when I first met them? This is how the cloud people communicate. They don't talk like we do. They don't make a sound. They send their thoughts to one another. You "hear" the words in your head but not your ears.*

But, she said, *You're talking to me now. What do you mean?* Then I could see the expression change on her face. It was as if a light bulb went on. *Wait a minute. You're doing it right now, aren't you? You're talking in my head. I thought I was hearing you, but you're not speaking. Your talking inside my head. How are you doing that?*

I don't know, I said as I shrugged my shoulders. *It just comes naturally. Or maybe like I said, they just like me more and gave me the gift!*

Don't start that again, Megan came right back at me. But just then she heard, or rather received, a voice in her head saying, *It's okay. You can do it. Go ahead.* She turned to look beside her, discovering the gentle face of a cloud looking right at her. It was Zon.

I could tell she was confused, but Zon's face was so friendly and inviting. I could see her gradually begin to relax. Slowly, she smiled back at him. She was meeting a new friend. I remember what it was like when I first met Zon. It was such a great and comforting feeling. I was so happy for her.

Greetings, Zon said to a new friend. *My name is Zon. Are you Billy's destiny?*

Before she could answer, from behind her, I immediately blurted out, *Yuck! No! She's just a friend. A good friend, but destiny? Yuck! No!*

Zon laughed at his mistake and apologized to me and then Megan. I couldn't believe that Zon had said that. Of all the things he could have first said. Of course, that got Megan's curiosity.

What is a destiny? she asked.

Zon giggled and slowly answered, a bit embarrassed now at his mistake. *Well, it's kind of like what you would call a husband or a wife. It's a partner for the duration. Something like that.*

Megan burst into screams of laughter. *Wow. No way. No way.* She turned to look at me for emphasis.

I looked right back at her. *No argument here, Megan.* Then I turned to Zon. *That's okay. You had no way of knowing. It's a mistake any cloud could make!* I added with a big grin. *No, Zon, she's not my destiny, although she's okay.* I made sure I didn't look at her when I added that. *Her name is Megan. Oh, and Megan, this is Zon.*

Well, Megan. It's nice to meet you, and with a smile, added, *and sorry for my mistake. But I'm glad that at least you're okay.* He looked over toward me with a wink.

Never one to miss a chance to get back, she responded. *No problem. People mistake me for Billy's destiny all the time!*

With that, I dove for her, but she floated away before I could get close. For a few moments, we forgot about the cloud people and resumed chasing one another until the rounds of laughter from the clouds got our attention. We slowed down and came back in front of Zon with an unofficial truce. That caused another wave of laughter from the clouds surrounding us.

Then suddenly, Megan looked at me. *Hey, wait a minute. I just realized that I'm doing it. I'm talking through my thoughts, just like you did. How did I do that? I didn't even think about. I just started doing it.*

That's what happened to me. I don't know how it works. It just happens.

Wow, that's cool, she said.

I told you that you could do it, Megan, Zon remarked. *It really is nice to meet you.*

With the initial meeting and introductions finally complete, Megan started asking Zon a lot of questions, pretty much the same ones I asked the first time we met. I was happy for her, but I think I was also happy for me. I was glad that I had someone to share this moment, yes, a witness, but also a friend. Having her with me reinforced what I always thought and wanted desperately to believe. This was real. As Megan continued firing questions at Zon, and he was answering, they were suddenly interrupted by a voice among the clouds.

One face moved forward and spoke. *Zon. I have a great idea. Since it's game day anyway, why don't we ask Billy and Megan to join us. They would be great at sevens!* Other voices joined in, agreeing with the idea.

You're right.

They would be good.

I want Megan on my team. She's fast!

Within seconds, all those gathered around joined in agreeing that it was a great idea.

You know, Bod, Zon said to the cloud that had made the suggestion, *you're right. That's a great thought. Let's do it. Let's have a game of sevens!* The whole gathering of cloud people erupted in applause. *Let's get started,* Zon announced.

I interrupted the cheers to ask the obvious question, *Excuse me, Zon. Could somebody please tell me what is sevens? How do you play?*

Zon laughed at his oversight. *Of course. I forgot you don't know how to play the game. It's really quite easy. You're going to love it. And I think you will both be great.*

Sevens

I had no idea what we were getting ourselves into. I couldn't imagine what kind of a competition clouds could have, but I couldn't help but get excited. The cloud people were so friendly, and I sensed that they loved to have a good time. I looked over at Megan and shrugged my shoulders.

So how about you? Do you think you're up for this, whatever this is?

You bet, said Megan. *I'm all in!*

With that, Zon called out for everyone's attention. *The first thing we're going to do is pick teams. Billy and Megan, since you're new, even though you're our guests, I won't ask you to be captains.*

Good idea, Zon. But wait a minute. Before we do that, can you please tell us what we're doing? What is sevens? How do you play?

Yea, what's the object of the game. What's the goal? Megan added. Again the whole group of clouds let out a cheer. It was obvious that this was a favorite.

After a few moments, everyone quieted down, and Zon resumed control. *First, we have to pick teams. This isn't a game that everyone can play, so most will have to watch.* Then looking at Billy and Megan, he said, *But don't worry. They love it. Even though most can't play, they still love the game. I guess it's a lot like some of your sports. Only some play, and the rest watch.*

You did say Megan and I could play, right?

Yes, Billy. Relax. You're both going to play. You're both in. Now for the captains, we'll have our two best players, Kon and Ton.

As if they anticipated that selection, they dashed right next to Zon. In unison they answered, *Ready when you are.*

With that, Zon looked at them both and said, *Pick a number.* It was obvious that they knew what that meant. Without hesitation, they both nodded as if to signal that they had already made their choice.

My number is three. What's your number? Zon asked.

Six, said Kon.

Four, said Ton.

Ton, you win, Zon announced. *My number was three, so you pick first—*

Wait a minute, I interrupted. *That's it? I mean nothing was written down. How do you know that's the number they picked? I don't get it.*

What do you mean? Zon asked. *They each thought of a number, and then they told me the number. Why is that so difficult?*

I hate to ask this, I said, *but what about cheating? How do you know that's the number each of you actually chose? I mean, couldn't one of you cheat, not that I think you would.*

Cheat. What is cheating? Zon asked with an obvious look of confusion. *I don't understand.*

Well, sometimes people will try to get an advantage. That's why we would write things down and use that as proof, I said.

Again that prompted a response from the clouds. There was an initial almost gasp and then a burst of laughter.

I don't quite get what you're saying. If I understand what you mean by cheating, we don't do that. It would be impossible for a cloud to cheat. We just don't do that. In fact, we don't even think about it.

I got a little embarrassed. I began to feel as if I had again insulted our new friends. Zon picked up on my embarrassment. Before I could say anything, he looked at me with such a kind face.

Forget about it, Billy. Don't worry. How could you know? It's just that us clouds are not exactly like you. So forget it and let's get back to sevens! As soon as he said that, all the clouds once more let out a big roar.

Since Ton had won the little game of "who picks first," he was ready to make his first selection. Just before he did, Zon leaned over to both Ton and Kon and reminded them that Megan and I would be playing. Then he got a little closer, and I heard him whisper to them. *You should know that Megan is a little faster!* Since they had played this game many times, it didn't take long to choose sides. While they were doing that, Zon turned to me and Megan.

Okay, now let me explain the rules to you. It's really very simple. We set up seven stations around a circle with the same distance between each station. Each team chooses one of their members to go first. Those two competitors go to the keeper—

I interrupted him, *Excuse me. What's a keeper?*

Well, that's kind of like one of your referees. They watch over the game and keep score.

Got it. Thanks, I said.

Zon then resumed his explanation. *They go to the keeper and whisper to him a number from one to seven. These two then go to the center of the circle. The second keeper—*

Wait a minute, I said, interrupting again. *A second keeper? Who is that? What's his job?*

I'm sorry, Zon said. *I have to keep remembering that this is completely new to you. Well, the second keeper has one important job that adds to the fun, which I will now explain. You'll see that he has to be a different person from the main keeper.*

Okay. I think I'm following you. Sorry to interrupt again. Go ahead.

The second keeper then announces a number from one to seven for all to hear. The difference between the number each competitor picked and the number that the second keeper announced is the number of stations each one must race to before returning to the center. The first one to reach the center wins the race—

Wait a minute, I interrupted again.

I know. I know, said Zon. *I was just about to get to that.*

You read my mind, I said with a big smile.

If the number that the second keeper announces is the same number as one picked by a competitor, then that's the number of stations to which he will have to race. Let's say I am competing, Zon continued to explain. *If I picked 2 and the second keeper calls out 6, then I have race to 4 stations before reaching for the center. If the second keeper calls out 2, then I only have to go to 2 stations since it matched my number.*

I got it, I told him. *That doesn't seem that difficult.*

It shouldn't be, Zon said as some of the clouds laughed. *But when you get into the heat of the race, it's easy to forget simple math!*

And that's it? I said.

No. No. There are still some more rules. During the race, if one competitor touches the other, or you might say, tags the other, that one must return to the center to begin again. Each competitor is allowed one tag or touch per race.

Well, what happens if they touch accidentally? I asked.

In that case, both have to return to the center. The main keeper makes that call. If there is any question, the second keeper can also make the call.

Okay, now it's starting to sound interesting. It's a little harder than I first thought.

Zon smiled. *It can get quite exciting.* Again all the clouds nodded their agreement. Zon then continued, *There are two different strategies. Sometimes a competitor may choose to go in the opposite direction of his opponent. That will avoid contact. Other times, he may choose to go the same way, especially if he has more stations to cover. That way, he can touch his opponent and send him back to the center.*

Megan then jumped in, *I think I've got it. I'm ready!*

Not so fast, Zon said to Megan. *That's great, but there's just one more part to the game. Each team consists of five members, and when each member of the team has competed, that completes one set. Five sets make up a game. The most races in one set wins the set, the best of five sets wins the game. See, it's easy—and a lot of fun!*

Suppose one team wins the first three sets? What happens then? I asked.

Well, game over. It's a shutout, but that has never happened. It almost always goes to five sets. That's what makes it exciting, explained Zon. *So are you ready?*

With an air of confidence, Megan announced, *Let's go. I'm ready. And I hope I'm up against you, Billy!* She pointed at me.

With a big smile, Zon announced, *That's exactly what we were planning. The two of you will be each team's anchor. This should be* real good!

Oh, yes it will. I can feel the victory already, I said as I looked at Megan. I have to admit that I was nervous. I already saw how well Megan could fly, but I couldn't let her know. I looked over at my team. *Let's get 'em!*

The teams were chosen, the circle of stations was set, and the two keepers took their places. With a roar from all the spectator clouds, the contest began. In short order, my team, or rather Kon's team, took a lead of two games to none, threatening exactly what I asked about—a shutout! Part of the reason, and I couldn't believe it, was that Megan had made a mistake in the last set, missing one of the stations by rushing to the center too soon. That error cost the team and put my side up by two with the opportunity to close out the game in the next set. However, it was not to be. Just as Zon had predicted, there was no shutout that day. Ton's team came roaring back, winning the third set easily, and the fourth one barely, each time with Megan being the hero. The stage was set for a dramatic fifth set.

I couldn't believe it. I just learned this game, and I was hooked. I looked over at Megan and could see the intensity in her face. She was as wrapped up in the competition as I was. The cloud people were right. This was a great game! I felt like I was in the Super Bowl in the fourth quarter with the game tied. My heart was pounding. I didn't know it at the time, but that game with their two new human friends would be remembered as one of the greatest games of sevens ever played.

I should have known. It almost seemed like destiny, but with tense and close races in the previous sets, it was a tie. It came down to Megan and me for the last set. We would determine the outcome. The pressure was unbelievable. I don't know if I ever wanted to win a competition more than I did that one. I was as ready as I could be, and I'm sure Megan was too. As if the tension wasn't thick enough, as we were ready to go to the center to await the start, Zon announced that because it was such a close game, a rarely used rule was put into effect. This rule stated that rather than whispering their number, each contestant would announce it out loud. We would also pick a number to determine which would announce their final number first. Megan won the choice and excitedly raced to the center post. I followed, a little nervous, but determined to win. All the clouds were cheering and yelling. I never imagined that clouds could make so much noise! I realized that by now, each of the spectators had not only a favorite team, but also a favorite human. They were rooting for their team, but also their new friend. It was so cool.

The signal was given by the main keeper, and Megan announced her number, *Three!*

I took a little extra time, although I knew that I had to make my choice before too long or forfeit. Giving it as much consideration as I could, I finally shouted out my selection realizing how important it was, *Two!*

The stage was set, and it was time for the second keeper to announce *the* number. This could determine the outcome, so there was an air of excitement and tension. Realizing the drama of the moment, the second keeper paused a little longer. In a loud and theatrical voice, the final number of was announced, *Six!*

Megan was thrilled because that gave her the advantage. I was really worried but tried to reassure myself. After all, it was only a difference of one. I figured I could make that up with quick turns but also knowing that I had the option of a touch. That could only be used once, so I would have to wait for the right moment. As it turned out, that rule would lead to the most exciting finish many had ever seen. The time had come. We were both ready, and then, finally, the keeper shouted, *Begin!*

As we began the deciding race, we chose to go in opposite directions. We passed our first station at exactly the same time. We dashed to the second, each of us one glancing at the other to check on their progress. Again we reached our second station at the same time. At that point, Megan had a clear advantage. With a difference in her number and that of the second keeper of only three, that left her with only one more station before heading for center. I still had two to go. Clearly, I had to do something, or I would easily lose. As I headed for the third, I managed to get a burst of speed and got just a little ahead of Megan, but I needed to do even more. Somehow, I managed to pass my third station and was on my way to the fourth just as Megan reached her third and final station. The whole game came down to this. All she had to do was dash to the center to win. She was heading down the final stretch and victory when I was able to swing myself around my fourth and final station to head for the center. She was just ahead of me and reaching for the center and the win. I still don't know how I did it, but I managed to stretch out my right hand and glanced the bottom of Megan's right foot. It was close, but the keeper announced that it was a touch, and Megan was now obligated to begin her run again. With me just behind her, all I had to do was touch the center, and I would be the winner. I was certain I was about to win. I had made a spectacular move and snatched victory out of the jaws of certain defeat, or so I thought.

Once again, this was a game of firsts. What happened next had never happened before, and I still can't believe it. Looking back, I could see that it was possible in theory, but for some reason, it had never occurred. From that time on, it would be known as a double-touch and became a regular strategy in every game. I'm still not sure if what happened next was quick thinking or instinct, but it was an obvious move once revealed. Without stopping to think or be disappointed at what happened, Megan dove to the center ahead of me to begin her penalty lap but, in the same motion, reached back to touch me as I was diving for the center. It was, indeed, a double-touch. At the same time, as she touched the center with her extended right hand, she reached back with her left foot and touched my arm. It happened so quickly I wasn't sure if it counted. Any doubt I had was immediately taken away as the keeper announced, *Touch!* I hung there for a moment in disbelief. I was so close to victory, but now I was touched and had to begin again. Megan didn't miss a beat. She was already well on her way to completing her penalty lap. Technically, it wasn't over, but it would take a miracle to pull this one out. I had already used my touch, so it came down to pure speed.

I took off after Megan trying to catch her. I gave it my best, but I had too much ground to cover. After the famous double-touch, Megan took off like a flash and had already passed her first station before I regrouped and took chase. Besides, she really was faster than me. In the end, it was a victory as much of strategy as it was speed and skill. As Megan reached the center, her fellow cloud teammates surrounded her. The excitement of their "group hug" was felt by all. The whole atmosphere erupted with cheers and shouts. Moments later, I reached the center, so disappointed. I really felt as if I had just lost the Super Bowl.

Much to my surprise, my cloud mates also gathered around me and gave me a "group hug." They cheered as loudly for me as Megan's team had cheered for her. Megan also came over and gave me a big hug. She whispered, "Wow. That was close."

I just couldn't be upset. The moment was so thrilling, and everyone was simply enjoying a great contest. I put my hand on Megan's shoulder and smiled at her.

"It sure was. I gave it my best, but that was a great move. Congratulations." After I paused a moment, I leaned over and added, "I guess you really are faster…but only a little!"

We looked at each other with a big smile and gave each other a huge hug. We raised our hands together in celebration of a great game. It there was an announcer, I'm sure he would have said, "The crowd is going wild!" As the excitement of the moment ran through us and the roar of the cheering crowds filled our heads, we both closed our eyes to take it all in.

The Next Day

The next thing I saw as I opened my eyes was my own room. I just lay there for a few moments to get my bearings. The sun was pouring in through the window. It was a beautiful day, and I felt so rested. I hopped up out of my bed and ran over to the window. As I looked out at the sunny day, I started thinking about last night. That was really intense! It was even better than my first night, and I was so happy that Megan was there too. That proved to me it was not just dream, and I could honestly say that I didn't even mind losing.

As I stood by the window thinking, I could hear noises come from the next room. I guessed that Megan was awake. I wondered what she was thinking. As I thought about what was going through her mind, I heard a tapping at my door. It had to be her. I heard a soft whisper.

"Billy. Are you awake? Get up. Open the door. Can I come in?"

I could hear the excitement in her voice. I went over and let her in. As soon as I did, she quickly stepped in my room and closed the door behind her. She studied my face for a moment as if she was wondering what I was thinking. Then as if she couldn't hold it in anymore, she blurted out. "Was that real? I mean were we flying? You were there, right? I mean you really were there? I wasn't dreaming?"

I let her wait for a few seconds, but I was about to burst. "Wasn't that the best?"

Without warning, she shrieked at the top of her lungs. "I knew it. I knew it. So cool. Wow, that was the best!"

I don't think she realized how loud she screamed, but everyone came running into my room, obviously believing that something was wrong. By the time they came in though, Megan had grabbed my arms and started jumping up and down.

"I knew it. I knew it had to be real!" With that, she let go of my arms, oblivious to the others in the room and jumped up on my bed. She started bouncing up and down as if she was on a trampoline. With her hands raised above her head, she kept saying, "Yaba daba doo! Yaba daba doo... I can't believe it. I went flying. I went flying. They're real! They're real!"

"What's going on?" Grandpa asked. "What's all the excitement? Not only did we hear you, but I think the Stetsons did too."

The Stetsons were their neighbors, and they were about two football fields away! I don't think Megan realized how loud she was. She could hardly contain herself. Finally, Grandpa's question sunk in, and she stopped jumping up and down enough to answer, "Oh, sorry. It's just that I went"—she paused for a moment and resumed jumping up and down again as she finished—"flying! I went flying last night! I met the cloud people. They are so cool. It was great!"

"Okay," Grandpa said, "calm down. Besides, you don't want to break Billy's bed." He looked over at me.

That still didn't stop her. "And I won. I won. That was the greatest race ever!"

I don't think she would have stopped jumping if Uncle Frank didn't go over to her and gently grabbed her as her feet hit my bed one more time. He put his arms around her and held for a moment until she finally stopped jumping. I was surprised that Uncle Frank could be that gentle. As he continued to hold her, he was saying, "Okay, Megan. Okay. Settle down. Settle down. Let's go down to breakfast, and you can tell us all about it."

"Good idea," said Grandpa.

And in typical fashion, Grandma joined in the encouragement, "I want to hear all about it, but please Megan, don't start jumping up and down at the breakfast table!"

"Hey, good one, Grandma," I said.

That and Uncle Frank's holding on to her finally settled Megan down. At last, she wasn't jumping. Then without warning and for no reason, she started crying. "Oh, I'm sorry. I didn't mean to get so carried away. I couldn't help it."

Grandma came to the rescue and took Uncle Frank's place. As only she could, she reassured Megan. As she slowly stopped sobbing, I went over to her and patted her on the head.

"Come on, champ. Let's go eat! Playing sevens makes you hungry."

With that, she gave everyone a big smile. "Okay," she said.

But as we all walked downstairs, she couldn't stop talking. The words were coming out so fast that it was hard to keep up. I looked at Uncle Frank, and he and I both smiled at one another. Even Grandma couldn't help but laugh. When we got to the bottom of the steps, Grandpa, Grandma, and Uncle Frank turned to go into the kitchen. Megan grabbed my arm and pulled me toward the front door.

"Come on. Let's go outside. I just have to look at the sky."

I didn't want to disappoint her, but I had to tell her. "Look, Megan. I already looked out my window. The sky is clear. I didn't see any clouds."

"Really? Are you sure? Let's look anyway. I have to see for myself."

Just as we were about to go out onto the porch, Grandma called from the kitchen. "Hey, kids, it's going to be a simple breakfast. Just cereal and muffins."

As we stopped, Megan called out, "Your corn muffins?"

"Yes, dear," replied Grandma.

I answered for both of us, "Okay. We're coming."

Even the lure of Grandma's corn muffins couldn't stop Megan though. "This will only take a minute. Come on. Let's go."

I couldn't resist. She had such a hold on my arm and was already pulling me out the door. She was determined. She pulled me out onto the porch and then down the steps and into the yard. The trees around the house hid part of the sky, but we could see enough to confirm my observation with Megan. It was a perfect day, if you weren't looking for clouds. I could see the look of disappointment on Megan's face, but she wasn't giving up.

"This doesn't mean anything. They may have just left. Yea. That's it. They had to go." Neither of us noticed that Uncle Frank had followed us and was standing quietly right behind us. He had heard enough of the talk on the stairs and in the yard to figure out what was happening.

Just then, Grandma's voice came through the open windows from the house. "Come on, you three. Let's eat. The table's set."

We were just about to go in, knowing that we didn't dare delay in responding to her announcement, when Uncle Frank stopped. "Hey, wait a minute," he said. "Look over there. I mean way over there. What do you see?" He was pointing out to the west of the house. There was a clearing between the trees, and we could see a good patch of the sky. It was blue, but suddenly, we both noticed at the same time. There was an unmistakable clump of white clouds off in the distance. At the same time, we turned to look at each other with wide open eyes.

"Do you think it's them?" Megan asked.

"It has to be," I said. "It has to be."

We then saw Uncle Frank squinting as he strained his eyes to see. He just mumbled as if too himself. "I wonder. Is it possible?"

As each of us were momentarily caught up in our thoughts, we were now interrupted by Grandpa standing on the porch. "What are you three doing? You've been called twice, and Grandma's waiting. Let's go. You don't want me, and I mean you don't want to get in trouble, do you?" he asked with a smile.

Of course, we wanted to stay outside a little longer and look at the clouds, but we knew Grandma was waiting. "Okay, Grandpa. We're coming," I said.

One by one, we walked past Grandpa as he quietly shook his head. Just as Uncle Frank walked by, I turned and saw Grandpa step off the porch and look in the same direction that we had been looking. I saw his eyes pop open a little. He just stood there for a second and slowly rubbed his chin as he turned to walk inside. As he turned to walk in, he saw all three of us looking at him. He knew we had caught him doing what we had been doing. He just smiled one more time. "Never mind. It's time for breakfast. We'll talk about it later."

Everyone grabbed their choice of cereal and one of Grandma's muffins. We sat down to eat, but before eating, we remembered the rule in Grandpa and Grandma's house. Even before breakfast, they say grace. As soon as the prayer was finished, we started talking. Megan started by sharing her experience last night. Once she got going, it was hard to interrupt, but everyone eventually managed to jump in. Within short order, each of us was asking questions and telling of our experiences with the cloud people. We were comparing notes and descriptions. Grandpa seemed particularly fascinated and asked Megan and me a lot of questions. As we rambled on, I looked over at Grandma. Suddenly, I realized that she was the only one who had not had any experience with the cloud people. She wasn't talking but seemed to be taking it all in. I started to wonder if she felt left out, but the expression on her face told me that she was enjoying our conversations and content to just listen.

She was the only one who had never seen the cloud people, so I never imagined that she would be the one to ask *the* question. I don't think she was doubting us, and I'm sure if she knew how much it would disturb us, she never would have asked it. I think she was just genuinely curious, and later, I was surprised that none of us thought of it before.

"Billy. Megan." It took a few seconds, but she eventually got our attention. Now that she had it, she paused, and then continued, "I can't help but ask. If it was nighttime, how could you see? Wasn't it dark?"

That's all she had to say. Megan stopped talking and looked off into the distance with a look that revealed what she was thinking. I must have had the same look, and I'm sure we were both thinking the same thing. I know she didn't mean it, but Grandma had presented us with a big challenge to our experience. I couldn't help but question myself. How did I see last night? How is that possible? Everyone had stopped talking, and Grandpa and Uncle Frank both looked at us. I'm sure they were concerned that we might be upset, but I also think they were waiting for our answer.

As I struggled to come up with an answer, Megan finally broke the silence. Almost defiantly, she blurted out, "No. It couldn't have been a dream. It was real. I don't know how we could see at night, but it had to be real. It just was."

Her speaking up helped rally my thoughts. I jumped to her defense. "It was exactly like the other night. Yea, it was night, but so what? I don't know how, but I could see fine. Remember, the cloud people don't communicate by talking. They just throw their thoughts or something like that. Why can't they make it feel like the sun is out? After all, we have lights that make it bright at night!"

"That's right, Billy," Megan added. "Just because we can't explain it doesn't mean it wasn't real."

Looking back, I'm not sure if we were trying to convince Grandma or ourselves. She had no idea that her simple question would cause such anguish. She was now clearly sorry that she had upset us, especially Megan.

"I'm sorry. I wasn't questioning you or what you were saying. I wasn't implying anything by it. It was just a question. I was curious."

"Oh, Grandma. Don't worry. We know that. Besides, as I think about, it is an interesting question. There's a lot about this whole thing I don't understand. I just know what I saw and what I, I mean"—I looked over at Megan—"*we* experienced."

Uncle Frank believed in the cloud people, but he was a committed skeptic. He was by nature a realist and one of those who always questioned things. "Look, guys. I know these things are real even though I still don't understand what they are. I've got to be honest with you guys. I'm not so sure about this flying stuff. You have to admit, Grandma asks a good question. Since it was night, how could you see? It had to be a dream." He didn't sound like he was arguing with us. I think he was just being Uncle Frank. He was trying to figure out the whole thing.

Megan didn't say anything. She just put her head in her hands and started to sob. Uncle Frank went over to her and put his hand on her shoulder. "I'm sorry. I wasn't challenging you. I'm just trying to understand. I believe you. I trust you, but I just don't get it." Then after a pause, in typical Uncle Frank fashion, he added, "Come on, Megan. Flying? Really? It just can't be. Besides, why don't you guys fly during the day? If you go during the day, I'd love to join you!"

He managed to bring a smile to Megan's face. She lifted her head out of her hands and looked at Uncle Frank with a grin. "Well, Uncle Frank, some people have it, and some don't."

Uncle Frank smiled back. I'm not sure if he was impressed with Megan's comeback, or if he was just happy that Megan seemed to feel better. It was just at that moment that a thought suddenly came to me.

"Hey, wait a minute, everybody. I just thought of something. Okay, I get it that you can't understand how we could fly or how we could see as if it was daytime, but what about this? How could Megan and I feel the same thing? If it was a dream, how could we be in it together and experience the same stuff?"

Now Megan sat up straight with her eyes wide open. "Hey. That's right! How could it be? Answer that, Uncle Frank!"

Grandma stood up to clean the table but paused to look at Uncle Frank. "They have a point, you know. How do you explain that?"

Before he could answer, Grandpa joined the debate. Perhaps as a distraction, but probably more out of curiosity, he asked us, "Tell me again about this game of sevens."

With that, Megan started again to excitedly share about the dramatic game of sevens. As she talked, I interjected my comments. Together, we described the excitement of that contest. I don't know if that's what Grandpa had in mind, but we soon forgot about Grandma's question and were totally caught up in the excitement of sevens. As we continued to talk, I noticed Grandpa listening intently and then looking over at Uncle Frank. He had an expression on his face as if to say, "Are you getting this?" I wasn't sure what was on his mind, but Megan and I continued to talk about last night, and Grandpa and Uncle Frank continued to listen, pausing to exchange looks with each other.

Eventually, my curiosity got the best of me. I interrupted Megan and looked at Grandpa. "Excuse me, Grandpa. What's up?" What are you thinking?"

"What do you mean," he asked.

"Well, you and Uncle Frank keep looking at each other and nodding and smiling. So what's on your mind?"

Megan had stopped talking and turned her full attention to Grandpa. She supported my question. "Yes, what are you two thinking about?"

Grandpa smiled and then looked at Uncle Frank. "Well, kids, I have to admit I was also wondering about last night. Was it a dream? Was it real? How could you see, and well…what does it mean? I have been listening to the two of you. I don't know if this answers Grandma's question or not, but I've noticed that there is absolutely no difference between your stories. I have no doubt that you both experienced the same thing. Whatever it was, it couldn't be a dream. How could the two of you have the exact same experience if it was only a dream?"

Megan got a big smile on her face. I think she was relieved to hear that. Uncle Frank followed up, "I hate to admit it, but that makes me wonder. I mean two people can't have the exact same dream, and two people can't be in each other's dream. It doesn't answer all the questions, but whatever happened last night, it certainly sounds real."

With those words of affirmation from Uncle Frank, Megan gave a two-thumbs-up. I too was relieved because I was starting to have some doubts. Then almost as if a bell was rung, without saying a word, all of us stood up and walked out to the porch. Even Grandma managed to walk away from the table without picking up the dishes. As we walked out onto the porch, again in silence, we all looked up at the sky. Each of us was caught up in our own thoughts, and no one spoke.

Finally, it was Uncle Frank who broke the silence. "Well, I don't know about the rest of you, but I'm really glad we're going on that balloon ride. I can't wait."

I jumped off the porch and started running around the grass with my hands stretched out as if I was flying. Megan jumped down from the porch and did a cartwheel.

"That's right! I almost forgot," I said. "I have a feeling we're going to see them. I just know it!"

"I think so too," Megan added. "And I bet I see them first!' She looked at me with that big grin.

"Well, I sure hope so," replied Grandpa. "I can't take too much more of this mystery. I have to admit, until your visit, Billy, I haven't thought too much about these cloud people, but now I'm really starting to get excited myself. I feel like a kid again! I guess you're never too old for adventure!"

I couldn't wait for that balloon ride. I was beginning to feel as if I was on a quest. I wanted to prove to myself that all of this was indeed real. I know what I saw. I know what I experienced. Now I wanted to know for sure.

Waiting

Our balloon ride was still a few days away. I wanted it to be tomorrow. I didn't know how I was going to wait that long. I had totally convinced myself that this was the only way I could finally prove the existence of the cloud people and know without a doubt that it was all real. I kept trying to remind myself of Grandpa's advice about my feet and all that philosophical *agite* stuff, but it wasn't working.

Every other year I would have loved just spending time at their house without any problem. I felt bad, but this year, it just wasn't enough. I don't know if they had already planned it or if they came up with the idea to get my mind off the balloon ride, but Grandpa and Grandma arranged for a three-day trip to Indianapolis. It was only about two hours from their house, and I had never been there. I couldn't believe it, but when they mentioned it, I actually managed to get excited. They even made arrangements for Megan to join us. Their kindness in giving me a vacation within a vacation saved my mind.

Never having seen anything like Indianapolis, I didn't realize how much there was to see and do. It was not only a great three days, but it succeeded in taking my mind off the clouds for that time. On the first day, we went to White River State Park. The gardens were okay, but I really liked the zoo. Megan said she liked the gardens better, but the zoo was okay! The second day, we saw the Eiteljorg Museum of American Indians and Western Art. I could do without the art, but all the Indian stuff was cool. The last day was the best though, the Indianapolis Motor Speedway Museum. Even though I couldn't wait to get up in the air in a balloon, it was a thrill to see all that car stuff. The afternoon ended at an indoor go-kart park. I imagined that I was in the Indy 500. The only thing that bummed me out is that Megan beat me, again. Oh well.

I never imagined that I could have had that much fun, but I did. It was a great distraction and helped me relax. However, on the ride back to my grandparents' house, I had time to look out the window of the car. That started me all up again. I couldn't help it. Even though the sky was clear and no clouds in sight, I couldn't stop looking and thinking. I noticed Megan doing the same. At least "balloon day" was almost here.

I expected that when we got back home, I would have a battle to endure those final hours. I could hear Grandpa's voice in my head, *You're going to miss out on your own vacation.* This time, though, it would be Uncle Frank that came to the rescue.

Uncle Frank

As we were driving down Interstate 65, we passed a bad accident. It looked as if someone was hurt, and an ambulance was coming from the other direction. As we continued driving, Grandma looked back at us from the front seat. "Let's say a prayer. I think someone might need a blessing."

My grandparents were very religious, and we said a short prayer for God to help whoever might be hurt and for God to bless the EMTs. I know Uncle Frank wasn't so religious, but I noticed that even he bowed his head for a moment.

Just a short time after that, we approached a rest area. Grandpa pulled over to take a break. When we came back to the car, I noticed a helicopter flying overhead.

"I think that's a medivac helicopter," Grandpa said. As we looked up at the chopper and heard the "thump thump" of the blades, I realized, out of the corner of my eye, that Uncle Frank was standing as still as a statue. His eyes were glued to the helicopter, and he was frozen in position with a strange look on his face.

"What's the matter, Uncle Frank," I blurted out.

With that, Grandpa held his hand up and put the other to his lips. He leaned over and whispered, "It's okay. He'll be fine. Just give him a minute."

I didn't know what was going on, but I obeyed Grandpa. Finally, the helicopter was down the road and fading from sight. Uncle Frank snapped out of his gaze and started walking back to the car. I couldn't help staring at him, wondering what happened. By the time we got back to the car, he must have realized that we noticed his odd behavior. He opened the car door and paused for a second.

"Don't worry. I'm okay."

Megan couldn't let it go and had to ask. "What happened, Uncle Frank? What was that all about?"

He didn't answer but just silently got into the car. Grandpa came back to Megan and I and again whispered. "Uncle Frank flew helicopters in Vietnam. He doesn't like to talk about it. I guess he just had what we veterans call a flashback. It's all right. He'll be fine."

I knew he served in Vietnam but never knew much about what he did. I also hadn't heard of flashbacks and really didn't understand. From that day, I never looked at Uncle Frank in quite the same way. Once we were back in the car, there was an awkward silence for a little while. I think everyone was afraid to say anything. I looked over at Megan and shrugged my shoulders, putting my finger over my lips. She just nodded her head. I don't know if she understood either, but she knew enough to keep quiet.

After a while, Uncle Frank finally spoke. "Sorry, kids. I guess that must have seemed a little weird. I guess now's as good of a time as any."

I was afraid to say anything but decided to take a chance. "As good of a time for what?"

"That's when it happened. That's when I saw them?"

Now I was even more confused, but suddenly, Megan's face lit up. She looked over at me and then Uncle Frank. "You mean the cloud people? The helicopter has something to do with the cloud people?"

He didn't answer at first, but just nodded his head. The car fell silent again, and we waited for him to continue. I didn't want to push him, but I couldn't wait to hear his story. At last, he seemed ready to continue.

"You see, Billy and Megan, I served in Vietnam. My job was to fly helicopters. I lost track of how many missions, I mean times, I flew, but it was a lot. When I saw that helicopter, it brought it back to me. My main purpose was rescue, kind of like that guy."

"Wow, Uncle Frank. That's cool! I never knew that," I said.

"Well, I really don't like to talk about it, but I know I freaked you out back there, so I figured I owed you some explanation. Anyway, it was during one of those missions that I met the cloud people."

Now he really had my attention. I did want to find out more about what he did, but I really wanted to know how he met the cloud people. I let the war stuff go and asked him, "So what happened? How did you meet them?"

Megan jumped right in, "Yes, Uncle Frank. Tell us. Please. I've got to hear this."

I think our curiosity about the meeting of the cloud people helped Uncle Frank relax. I could even see his face finally showing a little smile. He was starting to look like Uncle Frank again. He was ready to talk, and we were ready to listen when I realized that we were pulling into the driveway of Grandpa's.

"Sorry, kids. You're going to have a wait a little longer. We're home!"

As we parked, Grandma looked back at us. "I'll tell you what. Let's get our stuff out of the car and into the house. Then you and Uncle Frank can sit on the porch and talk. I'll get dinner ready. How does that sound?"

"You're the greatest, Grandma," I said as I jumped out of the car to unload.

In short order, everything was in the house, and Megan and I went to sit on the porch. Uncle Frank was already sitting. He beat me to the rocking chair! Well, since he was the guest speaker, he deserved it. After a few moments and before he started talking, Grandpa came out and joined us.

Not giving Uncle Frank a chance, I couldn't wait. "Okay, Uncle Frank. Let's have it. What happened?"

He couldn't help but smile and then began. "All right Billy. Here it goes. As I told you, I flew helicopter rescue missions. This one day was a day a lot like today. It was mostly clear and hot. Vietnam was usually hot. Let's just say it was a bad part of the war, not that any part was good. We got a call that one of our companies along what they called the Ho Chi Minh Trail was trapped by over seven hundred North Vietnamese. They were surrounded and pretty much doomed. Our job was to try to get them out."

I just sat there with my mouth open. I couldn't believe this was Uncle Frank. I never imagined him being a part of something like that.

"Did you save them?" Megan asked. "What happened?"

"Let's just say the enemy wasn't too happy about what we were doing. As we came flying in, they were doing their best to stop us."

"How, Uncle Frank? What did they do?"

Looking back, I realize that it was a kind of dumb question, and maybe that's why he paused.

"Well, Billy. They were shooting at us. They were shooting at us a lot. In fact, it was so bad I had to pull out. I didn't know what I was going to do. I had to get back and get those guys out." He stopped for a moment, then continued, "That's when your friends came to the rescue."

"You mean, the cloud people?" Megan asked as she stood up. At that point, she was not only standing but leaning toward Uncle Frank. I stood up also in anticipation of what he was going to say.

"Like I said, it was a clear day. No clouds around anywhere, at first."

"What do you mean at first?" I asked.

"I couldn't waste time, so without thinking, I turned to go back. That's when, out of nowhere, a huge bank of clouds came floating in. I was trying to figure out where they came from when right in front of me, I saw a face, yes, a cloud face. I couldn't believe it and thought that all the pressure was making me crazy. Before I could think any more, that face in the clouds starting acting like one of my officers. He began making motions with what looked like his arms as if he was directing the others—"

"You mean there were others?" I interrupted. He gave me a look as if to say, "Let me finish." With that, I bowed my head a little. "Oh, sorry. Go on."

He just smiled and then continued, "There were a ton of other faces in the clouds around me. As that one cloud began making motions, the others swarmed around my helicopter and made it almost impossible to see. Then that same face pointed what seemed like a hand at me to motion to follow him. By instinct, although not really knowing what I was doing, I followed him. We dove down, and I heard bullets flying, but nothing was hitting. Suddenly, there was the ground, and I could see some of our guys. I didn't even think. I quickly landed the Huey and called to the soldiers to start getting on board. In a split second, I was full and immediately pulled up. As I did so, I was enveloped in a dense fog, really a bunch of the cloud faces, so close to one another that it looked as if they were squeezing one another. I flew up and then, suddenly, was above the clouds. The air was clear. Without thinking, I made a beeline for the drop-off zone. As soon as I emptied the chopper, I lifted back up off the ground. I returned, only to find myself again surrounded by a thick cloud. I still can't believe it, but that happened three times. I never spoke to any of those clouds but did see their faces. Whatever they were, or are, they were helping me."

"Did you get them all?" Megan asked as Uncle Frank finished.

When she asked the question, he froze again. He did not answer right away. He at first looked away and then bowed his head. "Almost, Megan. Almost."

Realizing that maybe she shouldn't have asked the question, Megan said, "Oh, I'm sorry, Uncle Frank."

"That's okay," he reassured her. "All I know is that if it wasn't for those cloud people, I don't think we would have been able to get any of them."

I waited a moment, and then I just had to ask. "What about the other pilots? What about the other helicopter guys? Did they say anything? I mean, did they see any cloud people?"

"Believe it or not, no one said anything, and I never asked. Actually, your grandfather was the only one I ever spoke to about what happened."

Just as he said those words, Grandma came out on the porch. "Dinner's ready."

I have to admit I was hungry, but I was still so caught up in Uncle Frank that I wasn't quite ready. It didn't matter though because Grandma had spoken. One by one, we got up to go inside. Uncle Frank leaned over to help Grandpa off his chair. I started to go inside, and Megan ran over to Uncle Frank. She gave him a big hug. She held him tight for a few moments and then, finally, slowly pushed away.

"Thanks," that's all she said, and then turned to go inside.

"Yea, Uncle Frank. Thanks for telling us." I didn't know what else to say and also went inside.

Uncle Frank was left by himself on the porch for a moment. As I went in the door, I saw him walk off the steps and look up at the sky for a moment. Then he too turned to join us.

I enjoyed the food in Indianapolis, but nothing could compare with one of Grandma's meals. That night, she made meat loaf, and it was great. However, the dinner was quiet for a while. I was glad that Uncle Frank told his story but also felt bad that he had to talk about some of that stuff. I really didn't know what to say.

It was Uncle Frank himself who finally spoke. "Hey, Billy. Once you finish eating, you better check the weather. Remember, tomorrow, we're going up in the balloon!"

With that, the ice was broken, and the table erupted with our usual laughter and conversation. We talked about our trip to Indianapolis but ended up as it seems we always did on that vacation with talk about the cloud people. But finally, balloon day was here!

After dinner, of course, I had to check the weather one more time. Still looking good! As excited as I was, somehow, I managed to get to sleep that night and stay asleep! No adventures, no flying, no cloud encounters, just sleep. Even the next day ended up being just a regular day on vacation, waiting for the evening.

The Balloon Ride

When we arrived at the small airport where we were going for the balloon ride, Megan and I jumped out of the car as soon as it stopped. Uncle Frank leaned out the window and yelled after us.

"Guys. Wait a minute. We have to go into the office first to sign in."

We stopped running and came back to the car, letting him know that we didn't see any balloons.

Uncle Frank just smiled and shook his head. "Don't worry. You will."

Grandma and Grandpa then got out of the car. "Well, here we are. I haven't felt this excited in a long time. I can't believe it."

"Hey, Grandma, are you going up too?" I asked.

She just laughed. "I'll be very happy to watch from down here."

In the meantime, Uncle Frank got out of the car and went over to the office, a small building near one of the hangars. Above the door was the picture of a balloon and the sign: FLIGHT DREAMS. That was an interesting name for the company considering all the conversations we had about dreams. As we all walked in, there was a pleasant man behind the counter, talking on the phone. I assumed that was Gus, the guy Uncle Frank told us we were to meet. As he continued his conversation, he glanced up at Uncle Frank and held up a finger, clearly meaning he would be with him in a minute. As Gus continued his phone conversation, Megan and I looked around at the pictures on the walls. There were dozens of photos of balloons in flight and just as many of people standing in the balloon either just before or just after it had taken off into the air. I was getting more and more excited, and I could tell so was Megan.

Finally, Gus hung up the phone and came over to the counter. "Good evening, folks. So are you ready for your flight?"

Before Uncle Frank could answer, Megan blurted out, "*Yes*!"

"Well, I guess that answers that." Looking at Uncle Frank, he said, "You look good, Frank. Gosh, I haven't seen you in a couple of years. How have you been?"

"Oh, fine," Uncle Frank said. "It's good to see you too. I guess it's been a while. Thanks for fitting us in. Besides, I don't know what we would do with these two kids if we couldn't go up!"

Now that he and Uncle Frank had exchanged their greetings, it was time to get down to business. Gus looked down at us from behind the counter, "Well, I guess we better get you ready for your flight!"

With that, he brought out a form, and Uncle Frank quickly filled it out. As he was finishing, Gus looked up at the rest of us. "So how many of you are going? We have plenty of room."

Megan and I immediately raised our hands as if he didn't know we were going. Following our lead, Grandpa also raised his hand as if he was a kid back in school responding to the teacher.

"Yes, sir. Me too!"

Grandma then made it official. "No. Not me. I'm staying right here on the ground."

"That's fine, Ma'am," Gus said. As he said that, another man walked into the office. "If you'd like, you can ride with my coworker Tom in the chase vehicle."

"Chase vehicle? What's that?" she asked. "Well, we never know exactly where the balloon is going to land, so we need to have a way of getting back. The chase vehicle follows so we can all return here."

"Don't know where you're going to land? My goodness! Now I'm really glad I'm not going," she added.

That gave Gus and Tom a good laugh. "We don't exactly have a steering wheel in these things, but we know what we're doing. We'll get everyone up and down real safe."

"Never mind that," Megan said, interrupting the discussion. "We want to see clouds. I want to get right up to them."

"That's right," I added. "We want to see clouds."

"Clouds?" asked Gus. "That's odd. Most people want to avoid clouds. They're more interested in looking down below."

"Oh, that's boring," I said. "Nope, it's clouds we want to see."

"Well, I don't want to disappoint you, but have you looked up? There aren't many clouds. In fact, we prefer it that way. We need a clear sky. We can't go up if there are too many clouds. We have to be careful, and we must avoid storms." I guess our disappointment showed on our faces, so Gus immediately added, "But we'll see what we can do." He paused a moment. "By the way, why the interest in the clouds? What's so special?"

That question caught me off guard, and I quickly looked over at Megan. What should we say? I felt a little embarrassed. There was no way we could say anything about what we were really up to. Fortunately, Megan responded, "Oh, we just like clouds. We're studying them in school, so we thought it might be cool to see them up close." She secretly looked over at me and gave me a wink.

I jumped to support her. "That's right. We just thought that would be interesting since we have been studying them." Then to make sure I covered myself, I added, "But sure, we also want to look around, just like everybody else. Besides, there's nothing odd about looking for clouds though."

Megan gave me a look as if to say, "What are you doing? Let it go!"

I realized that I was overselling. "I just want to go. I can't wait!"

"Great," Gus said. "Let's go ballooning?"

"All right!" Megan and I said in unison.

"Do I need a jacket?" Grandpa asked. "I don't want to get chilly."

"You can bring one if you want, but you'll be fine. It's a beautiful evening."

With that, we all went outside and walked a short distance to a field near the airport. By the time we got to the spot where Gus was standing, Tom had pulled up in a big SUV. He jumped out, opened the back, and said, "Here it is!"

He and Gus pulled out a large basket and what looked like a huge ball of canvas. Next, they brought out a big fan. Within minutes, they had the canvas stretched out on the ground. It looked like it was almost one hundred feet, though I'm not really sure exactly how long it was. Tom started the fan, and the big balloon began to inflate. I was amazed at how quickly it expanded. After a while, when the balloon was pretty full of air, then came the really cool part. Gus lit up a gas blower, and there was a loud roar. Flames shot out, and the balloon gradually began to stand upright.

Then as if reading my mind, Gus looked at me and said, "Don't worry. We've done this plenty of times. No one gets burned!" Tom just smiled. I guessed that meant almost everyone worries about that their first time.

Even Grandma seemed fascinated with the whole process. Uncle Frank, who had been in a balloon many times before, enjoyed watching the expression on our faces.

"As many times as I've done this, I never get tired of the thrill of blowing up the balloon. Pretty cool, isn't it?" Gus asked.

"You bet," I said.

"It sure is," Megan added with excitement.

It's hard to believe, but I got so caught up in the preparation that for those moments, I forgot about our cloud search. Before too long, the balloon had taken shape and rose like an impressive monument right before our eyes. As it stood up right before us, suddenly, my eyes popped open and then my mouth. I couldn't believe it. The balloon was mostly blue, but right in the middle was a big smiley cloud face!

I wondered if maybe Gus knew something. Is it possible that Gus had seen the cloud people? Maybe Uncle Frank had told him about our experience. My heart started to pound, and I looked over at Megan and pointed to the balloon. From the expression on her face, it was obvious that she was thinking the same thing. She just nodded back at me. The balloon wasn't quite ready, so I figured I had a quick moment to ask a question. I didn't want to be too obvious so I tried to be casual.

"Hey, Mr. Gus. That's a really cool balloon. Why did you put a cloud face on it? I've never seen anything quite like it."

"Really?" Gus asked. "You've never seen a smiley face before?"

Everyone laughed, and I felt a little silly. Maybe Gus hadn't seen any cloud people. Maybe it was just a coincidence. Nothing in his expression let on that he knew anything. I was a little let down, hoping that cloud face meant something more to him.

"Actually, it was Tom's idea. We used to have just a blue sky and some clouds, but we get a lot of families, like yourselves, so he suggested the smiley face. He thought it would be good for the kids. So do you like it?"

Trying to hide my thoughts and not give anything away, I just went along with it. "Oh, yes. It's great."

It was obvious that Gus picked up on my disappointment, even though he couldn't know what I was really thinking. He just laughed and in an overly dramatic fashion responded, "Well, I'm glad you think it's absolutely fantastic," adding a little wink.

"Oh, sorry. No, it really is great. I just got distracted for a minute."

Megan fortunately jumped in at that moment. "Well, I think it's cool. Good design!"

"Well, if the art critic session is over, what do you say we go for a ride!" Gus said.

One by one, we got into the basket. Grandpa struggled a little but finally managed to get in without too much of a problem. Uncle Frank was the last one in. Surprisingly, with all of us on board, including Gus, there was plenty of room. Then all of sudden, almost without warning and with no jerks or bumps, we were slowly rising in the air. It was the coolest feeling. Moments before, we were on the ground talking, and now, we were just floating on air. My main goal was to see clouds, but I couldn't help gazing down at the ground as we continued to rise. When I looked down, there was Grandma smiling and waving. I could barely hear her as she shouted up to us, "Have fun! And don't forget to land safely!"

Within moments, we were floating a few hundred feet above the earth. It was a spectacular sight.

"This definitely beats flying in battle," Grandpa said as he looked at Uncle Frank.

"It sure does, Ace," Uncle Frank responded as he gave him a respectful salute.

"This is really neat," I said, and then without thinking, I added, "but it does feel different when you go this slow." As soon as the words were out of my mouth, I realized what I said. I looked nervously over at Gus to try to see if he noticed. There was no way I could tell him about my flying.

"What do you mean? Have you flown before? Don't tell me you were a fighter pilot too?" Gus let out a laugh as he looked at Grandpa and Uncle Frank.

"No, of course not. I was just imagining being in a plane," I said with a smile. I don't think Gus picked up on anything. Close call.

All the while, Megan was looking out at the horizon, hoping to see some clouds. She brought a small pair of binoculars with her, but I don't think they were very powerful. I should have brought Grandpa's big ones. Oh, well, too late now. After a few minutes of her unsuccessful searching, I asked her, "Let me have a look."

With no clouds in sight, she willingly gave up the binoculars. I quickly grabbed them and began searching the sky.

Gus leaned toward me and said, "You can see a lot more if you look down below. It's a really cool sight."

I lowered the binoculars to look at him. "Oh, thanks. I was just looking around. Thanks for reminding me."

Not wanting to take any more chances of letting Gus know my real intentions, I put the binoculars to the side and leaned over to look at the ground. As I did so, Gus turned to Megan.

"So you really want to see some clouds. For school, right?" Then he paused. "You must be good students," he added with a smile. I started to think that it wasn't going to be easy to keep searching the sky without letting Gus get suspicious. Till I could figure something out, I continued looking down below. In the meantime, I hoped that Megan would keep her eyes open for clouds.

As I continued looking below, I had to admit that it was pretty fascinating. After all, when I was floating around with the cloud people, most of my attention was on them, not the ground! Just at that moment, we were going over a house, and I could see the whole family in the backyard. They were obviously having a barbecue. As our balloon floated by, the entire group looked up and waved. As their voices faintly reached the balloon, all of us waved back.

"Hello down there!"

Gus interrupted our greeting. "From up here, we can hear them because their voices carry up, but they can't hear us. They can only see us. It's always fun watching people below. That's one of my favorite things about ballooning. Besides having fun, I feel as if I'm giving them a little thrill. After all, who doesn't like to see a big balloon with a smiling cloud face float over your house?"

As soon as he said that, we were now over a man and woman walking a dog in the woods behind their house. The dog was barking furiously. The two people were angrily waving for the balloon to keep going. Unlike Gus's assessment, they didn't seem very happy to see a big balloon with a smiling cloud face above them!

As we continued to glide along, a voice came over Gus's walkie-talkie. It was Tom in the chase vehicle. "Hey, Gus. You better keep moving. It's that couple again. You know how they hate balloons!"

"I know. It drives the dog crazy. I tried to avoid them, but the wind didn't cooperate. I'll be out of their way in just a few seconds."

As we floated past the unfriendly dog walkers, we then heard Grandma's voice on Gus's walkie-talkie. "Hello up there! How are things? I can see you. It looks like fun."

Grandpa asked Gus if she could hear him if he talked back on the walkie-talkie.

"Sure," Gus said. "It's all yours."

"Hi, dear. We're doing great. It's a fun ride. Wish you were here." It wasn't the time for a long conversation, but it was a lot of fun to connect for just those few moments. It made us feel as if Grandma was in the balloon with us.

Our balloon continued to float peacefully along. It was a perfect evening. I had almost forgotten about clouds and was really caught up in enjoying the feeling and the view. Megan, however, couldn't give up. She managed to glance below every now and then but spent most of the time searching the sky. By this time, she had reclaimed the binoculars and continued diligently searching for any sign of clouds. I hadn't planned it that way, but by talking with Gus, I managed to keep his attention away from Megan. That kept her free to keep looking. Even so, she did manage to keep a nice balance between looking around her for clouds and also checking out below to keep Gus from getting suspicious.

As we continued our trip, there was one moment that definitely grabbed our attention. We were approaching a group of trees, and it looked as if I could touch them. I panicked for a second, thinking we might crash. Just then, with his expert touch, Gus gave the burner an extra boost that lifted us in plenty of time to avoid actually striking the trees. It was close though!

As we safely floated past the trees, Megan suddenly began screaming, "Look. Look. Clouds. Over there. Over there!"

Her shout startled everyone. All of us turned to look in the direction she was pointing. I think she suddenly realized what she had done. She forgot she wasn't just with us. Gus was in the balloon. She felt a bit embarrassed and sheepishly looked at him.

"Sorry. I just got carried away. I didn't mean to shout."

"I know. I know," he said. "It's that darn school. They have you all hung up on clouds," he said with a wink. "I'll tell you what. I'll try to float closer to those clouds if you promise that you'll get a good grade!"

Megan seemed relieved that Gus just went along with it, but I think she was even more excited that we were actually going to get a closer look at some clouds. As we slowly drifted closer to them, the balloon became strangely silent. Each of us—Grandpa, Uncle Frank, Megan, and me—were all just staring at the approaching clouds. I think each of us forgot about Gus and weren't even worrying about what he might think. I wanted so badly to see cloud people, and I know Megan did. Every once in a while, one of us would gasp, thinking for a brief moment that we had seen something, but unfortunately, we didn't. Out of the corner of my eye, I noticed that even Gus was focused on looking at the clouds, even though I'm sure he wasn't looking for the same reason.

At one point, we seemed so close to clouds that I imagined I would actually be able to touch them. I even remember reaching my

114

hand out to try. I think we were all mesmerized when Gus broke the spell by saying, "You know what, clouds really are fascinating. I'm usually pointing things out for people to see below us. Now that I'm looking, I have to admit. They really are fascinating."

Grandpa nodded, but none of us spoke. We just kept staring at the clouds. As intently as we looked, there were no faces. No cloud people showed themselves.

We continued to float by them in silence as if held in a trance. Each of us continued the search, and I'm sure each one was hoping to be the first to spot one. As wrapped up as I was in the search, I realized that we were almost past that cloud formation. That meant my great balloon quest had failed. I was crushed and then looked over at Megan. I could tell by her expression that she was also bummed out. I looked at her and shrugged my shoulders. What could we do?

It was Gus who interrupted the moment with a dose of reality. "Sorry, folks. But our time is coming to an end. We have to get this thing down." Even with that, it was difficult to stop looking at the clouds and hoping. We had passed the clouds, and I could see that we were over a big clearing. "This is a perfect spot," Gus said.

Just then, Tom's voice came over the walkie-talkie. "Hey, Gus. You guys going to fly all night? You better take advantage of this field because if you don't, the next good spot is way down the road."

"Gotcha, buddy. I know. We're coming down.

With that, there was a big hiss as Gus let some air out of the balloon. It slowly floated down and the ground was getting closer and closer.

"Okay, everyone. Let's pay attention. We'll be down very shortly. Hold on to the side. There will be a slight jolt, but not too bad."

Right after he said that, the basket started brushing through the tall grass in the field. The grass acted like a brake, and we slowly came to halt very peacefully, right in the middle of the field. The basket slowly tipped over. Tom was already there and grabbed hold to stop the balloon from going any further. Gus jumped out and helped him secure the basket. Once it completely stopped, he first helped Grandpa out. After everyone was safely out, Gus and Tom got to work pushing the air out of the balloon.

"Need some help?" asked Uncle Frank.

"Sure," said Gus. "Just slowly crawl along and flatten out the balloon."

They lined up and methodically crawled up the balloon forcing the air out of the sides. Once I realized what they were doing, I didn't want to be left out. I jumped on top and joined the others.

"Okay, Billy. You can help. Just remember this isn't a trampoline! We have to push the air out, not bounce."

"Oops," I answered. "Okay. Got it."

With that, I threw myself carefully forward time and time again to push out the air. As I did so, suddenly to my surprise, I found myself right on top of the cloud face on the balloon. I paused for a moment and stopped working on deflating the balloon. My mind began to wander as I found himself right back into the world of the cloud people.

"Hey, Billy. How about helping?" teased Uncle Frank. "Let's earn your keep!"

I shook my head and laughed a little, realizing that I had started to daydream. I went back to helping to finish deflating the balloon. It wasn't as much fun as floating in the sky, but it didn't even seem like work.

As we were getting all the air out of the balloon so that it could be folded up, Megan was talking with Grandma. "Did you see any?" Grandma asked, knowing how much Megan was counting on seeing cloud people.

"No, Grandma. Not even one. We did get pretty close to one set of clouds, but no faces."

Knowing it was time for a little teaching, Grandma put her hands upon Megan's shoulders and looked into her eyes. "That's the way it goes. Life can be disappointing. We can't always see or have what we want. But tell me. Wasn't it fun anyway?"

"Well, kind of. I was mostly looking for them, but it was cool being up there. It was super peaceful."

"Well, I'm glad," said Grandma. "At least it wasn't a wasted trip."

"No, Grandma. It was okay." Then after a pause, she added with smile, "Thanks."

In the meantime, the balloon was not only flat, but Gus and Tom had it all bundled and back inside the basket. They were getting ready to lift it into the back of the SUV when Uncle Frank came over.

"Here, let me give you a hand." With one big heave, it was safely placed in the back of the vehicle.

"Nice work, guys," said Grandpa. "I love watching other people work!"

"This really isn't work," responded Tom. "We've done this so many times, it's hardly any effort at all. Most of all though, I just enjoy knowing that people had a good time. You did have a good time?" he said as he looked at me and Megan.

"Yes, we did," we answered together.

"Thanks. It was great," I added.

Gus was standing right next to us, so he could also see the expression on our faces. I guessed he knew we were a little disappointed but couldn't quite figure out why. I don't think he wanted to push the issue, but he seemed curious.

"Now you're both sure you had a good time? I mean, you look a little disappointed. I've had people who were a little scared, but I never had anyone who was disappointed."

Gus was such a nice man; I felt bad that I didn't come across as more grateful. Besides, it wasn't his fault that we didn't see clouds. He did his best, and it really was a great flight.

"Really, Gus. It was great. I was just hoping to see more clouds. Not just for school and all. It's just that I have this thing for clouds. I don't know what it is, but I've always been fascinated with them. I hoped we might see more, but that's fine. We did have a good time." I think that convinced him. That's good because I didn't want to leave him thinking he didn't do a good job.

"I'm glad," Gus said. "Well, I think it's time we get back."

Everyone squeezed into the SUV, and just like that, the adventure was over. We weren't too far from the airport, so it wasn't a long drive. I was going to look out the window for one last look at the sky, but it was getting dark. Yes, the great balloon day was over.

Surprise

When we arrived, Gus got out of the SUV first. "Well, folks, it's traditional to have a little snack after flying. We have some cheese and crackers and either champagne or sparkling cider."

A woman was waving us over to a picnic table near the office and under a tree. It was Gus's wife, and she had a simple but inviting display waiting for us as we came over.

"Isn't this nice," said Grandma. "Now I won't have to get supper ready!"

Instantly, Grandpa brushed up against Grandma. "Sorry, dear. This is nice, but it just won't do for us balloonists. After all, flying makes you hungry. Right, Gus?" he said as he looked over for support.

Gus was attuned to the interchange and wasn't going to spoil Grandpa's plan. "Sure. This is just an appetizer to hold you over until you get home to a nice cooked meal!"

With that, Grandpa smiled at Grandma as if to say, "I told you so." Grandma playfully punched him on the shoulder. "I know. I already had it planned. Don't worry. You won't starve!"

After enjoying the hospitality and good conversation, it was time to leave. Gus's wife, with the help of Tom, cleared the table. As they did so, Gus and the rest of us walked back over to the car chatting about our balloon ride. Even though we had just met, Gus and his wife and Tom seemed like old friends that we had known for a long time.

When we reached the car and were saying our goodbye's, I didn't imagine that I would ever see them again. What happened next though really took me by surprise and set the stage for our future relationship. Grandpa and Grandma were already in the car, and Uncle Frank had jumped into the driver's seat. Megan and I were standing by the back door. Part of me didn't want to leave, so I guess I was taking my time. We waved one last time.

"Thanks again," I said. "It was a lot of fun."

"Yea. It really was," added Megan.

Just as we were about to get in the car, Gus stepped forward, leaned over, and looked at us. As he did so, he whispered, "You've seen them, haven't you?"

Even Uncle Frank and Grandpa and Grandma heard him. Everyone froze for just a moment. The first thought that came into my mind was, *Did he really say that or did I imagine it? I mean, could it be?* I then wondered if everyone else heard. I quickly looked around, and it was obvious by the look on their faces that they had. Time stopped for a moment as the words sunk in. Before any of us could say anything, Gus helped end the suspense.

"I've seen them too," he said. "I could tell by the way you were acting. You've seen them, haven't you? I finally figured out that's why you were so interested in the clouds. And that face on the side of the balloon? I put that there because I've seen them. It wasn't Tom. It was me. I just wasn't sure at first. That's why I didn't want to say anything."

No one responded, so for a moment, I think Gus panicked that maybe he had misjudged his new friends and embarrassed himself. If he did panic, it didn't last long. Megan and I jumped away from the car and grabbed Gus's arms.

"This is great!" I blurted out.

Megan seemed a little more cautious but followed up. "Really? You're not just kidding, are you? I mean, seriously. You've seen them for real?"

"Yes, Megan. I really have. Like you were today, every time I go up in the balloon, I'm looking. I guess once you've seen them, you're hooked."

"What happened? When did you see them? Did you talk to them?" I asked.

By now, everyone was out of the car and had joined in the conversation. In short order, Grandma's dinner plans were put on hold. No one was thinking about eating now. In fact, it was a while before we finally broke up the discussion. Gus took a deep breath and started to answer our questions. That evening began a friendship that has lasted to this day.

"I haven't talked about this to anyone until now. I'm sure you can understand. Folks would think I'm crazy if I ever said anything so I just keep it all to myself. Only my wife knows, and as good a guy as Tom is, if I ever told him"—he glanced over toward his coworker—"he'd definitely think I was crazy. My wife, she already knows I am," he added with a smile. "Well, at least she believes me. So until I talked with you, she's the only one."

"I know exactly what that's like," I said. "Yes, I definitely do. I was so afraid when we were up in the balloon that you might figure something out. To think that I was afraid you would notice. This is so cool. So what happened? You were going to tell us."

"It was six years ago. I still remember the date, August 24. I was supposed to take a family of three for a balloon ride. It was the little girl's birthday. It was a perfect night for a balloon ride. I was looking forward to it because I love flying, but I really enjoy making kids happy. I got a phone call in the afternoon that they had to cancel. They were disappointed, and so was I. Well, it was a great night, and I was all set, so I decided to a take a ride anyway. I left from just about the same spot that we did early tonight. The sky was clear. In fact, I don't think when I took off that there was a cloud in the sky. Well, it was a typical flight. Everything was going fine, and I was just relaxing and enjoying the view and the quiet. I love being up there. I was up for about one-half hour when all of sudden, I saw this group of clouds getting close. It seemed like they came out of nowhere. As they got closer, I got a little worried that I might not be able to see or that I might get knocked off course. As the cloud formation was almost on top of me, I began to hear voices. I mean I couldn't exactly hear them. It's weird, but—"

I looked at Megan and she looked at me and before he could finish the sentence, we both said, "It was as if the words were in your head."

Gus stopped and looked at us. "That's right. That's exactly right. So you know. You've *heard* them too!"

"We sure have," I answered. All of a sudden, I began to feel like an expert on the cloud people!

"That's a relief," Gus continued. "I always knew what I saw, but I was never quite sure about the whole words in the head part. I didn't have anyone to talk with. Wow, this is great."

"What happened next?" asked Megan.

"Well, I didn't see any faces at first. I just heard the voices. I remember hearing numbers."

Again Megan and I looked at each other, "Sevens!"

"What did you say?" asked Gus.

"Never mind," Megan responded. "It's a game, but forget that. Go on. What happened? Did you ever see faces?"

"I know I was moving, but for a few moments, it felt as if the balloon was standing still. I couldn't figure out what was happening. I didn't know what I was hearing, and I didn't know where these clouds came from. Then all of a sudden, I saw a face in the middle of clouds, looking right at me. I just stared, and for those few moments, whatever I was looking at seemed as surprised to see me as I was to see him or it or whatever I was seeing.

"I couldn't believe it. I just stood there, completely forgetting about my balloon. Then I heard words in my head, you know, like you guys said—inside of me. 'Greetings,' the voice said. 'We've seen you up here before. We noticed your balloon many times before. I didn't think we would ever meet. We were never quite close enough.' Another voice then added, 'Yes, this time we were so caught up in our game that we didn't realize how near we were. Well. Here we are! Hello.'

"Not only was I confused at what I saw, but now it or him or they, were 'talking' to me. I just couldn't believe it. Whatever it was, it was smiling. It had such a nice face. I wasn't afraid, but I just couldn't make sense of it."

"That's what I felt the first time I saw one when I was on the plane coming out here. But now that I've met them and flown with them, I feel like they're among my best friends," I said.

"Wait a minute," replied Gus. "Fly? Did you say you flew with them? I thought this was your first balloon ride?"

Megan laughed. "Guess what? I've flown with them too, but not in a balloon. I mean we actually flew!"

Gus took a step back. I think he was trying to figure out whether we were playing a trick or if we were serious. Everyone else was following our conversation but not saying anything. As Gus was studying our faces, Uncle Frank stepped forward.

"Listen, Gus. They're telling the truth. Not only have they seen them, but so have I and Grandpa here. Now as for this flying with the clouds stuff, I'm with you. I'm not so sure about that. I personally think it was just a dream."

Gus turned to listen to Uncle Frank, and I think that now he was even more confused. Adding to his confusion, Megan jumped in again. "Don't listen to him. It wasn't a dream. It was real!"

That began a rather lively debate between Megan and I and Uncle Frank that left poor Gus on the sidelines as if he was watching a tennis match. I don't think he knew who or what to believe. A few times, he tried to intervene, but there was no stopping us. I know Megan and I weren't going to give in, and Uncle Frank, as much as we loved him, wouldn't either. I'm never sure though if he really means it or is just trying to get us going. At any rate, poor Gus, after finally meeting someone he could talk to about his experience, found himself in the middle of a great debate.

In the meantime, Grandpa and Grandma were leaning against the car as they took it all in. They looked over at Gus and just shrugged their shoulders. With that, Grandpa let out a little giggle, and that startled Gus. The next thing he knew, he was laughing out loud at the whole scene. In turn, that got even Grandma smiling. Their laughter managed to do what no comments had been able to do—stop the arguing. We suddenly realized that we had been so completely caught up in the debate that we forgot everyone else. Not only did we stop arguing, but we too started laughing. What just a few moments ago was a serious moment of revelation turned argument was now just one big laughing party.

Eventually, it was Uncle Frank who spoke. "Sorry, Gus. I guess we got carried away. We didn't mean to cut you off. Sorry." And because he always had to get in the last word, he looked at me and Megan, adding, "It's just that they were wrong, and I had to call them on it!" Before we could respond, he cleverly cut us off by immediately adding as he looked at Gus, "But please continue. We want to hear the rest of your story." He looked over at us with his usual taunting smile. Both our looks let him know, *This wasn't over!*

Gus took a moment to make sure that he actually had the chance to speak. Convinced that the debate had at last subsided, he seemed glad to pick up where he had been interrupted earlier. "Thanks, Frank. Well, that was interesting! I'm just glad that you all get along so well," he said as he offered a huge grin. "So as I was saying before the great dream debate, I still wasn't sure what I was looking at, and I certainly was not sure if it was real. I thought that I must be imagining the whole thing. I decided to take a chance and respond. 'Hello, my name is Gus. I've been ballooning in these parts for years, but I've never seen you. How can that be?' The face smiled. 'We like to keep to ourselves. We're afraid if people knew about us, our peaceful lives would be over. I can see you have a nice face. I can read faces and tell what kind of a person lies underneath. I know I can trust you. So I have to ask something of you. You cannot tell anyone about us. You must keep our secret. If people knew about us, it could ruin our lives. You would be overrun with people wanting to take balloon rides to come stare at us. We would be like exhibits in a zoo. We would lose our peaceful existence. You must not tell anyone about us. Can we count on you?'

"At first, I didn't know what to think or say. I wasn't even thinking about telling anyone. Besides, if I did, who would believe me? Most people would think I was crazy! Well, it was getting dark, and it was time for me to go down, but before I floated away, I had to ask one question. 'What about my wife? Can I tell her?' 'You mean your destiny?' 'My what?' I asked. 'Never mind,' came the reply. 'That's what your destiny, I mean your wife is for. To share with. That's okay.'"

"So you never told anyone besides your wife?" Megan asked.

"Have you?" Gus asked, turning the question right back at her. "Nope. I've never told anyone except my wife until today. I'm a man of my word. I gave my word that day, and I don't break my word." He looked back at his office and then leaned forward to whisper, "I haven't even told Tom. I remember his asking me at the time why I wanted to put the cloud face on the balloon. He said he liked it as it was. Fortunately, Tom accepted my explanation about doing it for the kids who come for rides. I think he even liked it once I told him that. I must admit I got a little nervous when you asked about the cloud face on the balloon. I was glad when you also accepted my reason too. But when you did ask, that got me thinking. First, the balloon face, and then your obsession with clouds got me suspicious. I know I took a chance when I spoke up, but I was finally convinced that you too had seen them."

"That's really something," I said. Then I had to ask, "Did you ever see them again? I mean you've been up here plenty of times. Surely you ran into them?"

"Nope. Never again," said Gus. "I admit that every time I'm up in the balloon, I'm looking, but so far, no luck. Not even close. That gave you away too, Megan. I know that feeling. I've scanned the skies the way you were today, always trying to not let people know what I'm doing. Yup. I know that feeling."

Megan smiled back. It felt good to have met someone outside of our circle who also knew the cloud people. It was more than just a confirmation of what we experienced. It was a relief to be able to talk to someone else about it. The cloud people never asked us to promise to never say anything, but somehow, we just knew that we had to keep it secret. It was an unspoken understanding. Meeting Gus and hearing him talk about keeping his word made me realize that day how important trust is to friendship. As we all became friends, we made a pact that we would each keep the secret.

Looking at me and Megan first and then Grandpa and Grandma and then Uncle Frank, Gus asked, "So what's your story. What did you see? What happened to you?"

I started, recounting my trip on the plane and then, one by one, each shared their encounters. By then, it was getting late, and I know I was getting hungry. The snacks were nice, but I wanted more! I wondered if Gus read my mind when he interrupted. "By the way, is anyone else hungry? What do you say we go grab a quick bite to eat? I know a quiet place where we can talk. Tom will take care of everything here."

"That sounds great," Uncle Frank said. "I'm starved."

With that, Gus went to find Tom to ask him to close up shop and tell his wife what we were doing. He came back and led us to a diner about a mile down the road. We got a table in the corner, away from everyone else, where we were free to talk. We sat there and picked up where we left off about the cloud people. The food came and we ate and we talked and talked and talked. I think we all lost track of time. I'm not sure how long we were sitting there, but finally, Grandma was the one to end the evening.

"I'm sorry to break this off, but we have to leave. Billy is leaving to go home tomorrow, so we have to get back."

That realization made my heart sink. This great adventure was just beginning, and now I was going home. My few days with my grandparents felt as if I had been there for months. I really didn't want it to end.

Grandpa, always the wise one, noticed the look on my face and figured out what was going through my mind. "Billy, remember what I said about keeping your feet on the ground? We can't live our whole life at once. It comes in stages. If we cram it all into one moment, that takes all the fun out of it. After all, what would be left?" he asked with a smile.

I wasn't really convinced but knew that I would eventually have to leave. I thought Megan was going to cry, but then she seemed to catch herself. "Hey, Billy. This isn't over. We'll talk on the phone. Besides, you're coming back next summer. Just think how great that will be!"

"I know," I said, "but it sure is going to be a long year."

Grandma had finally managed to get everyone back to the car. We were all inside except for Uncle Frank. He was talking with Gus. The two were whispering to each other. I wondered what they were talking about. Megan was by the window on their side, so I motioned to her to try to listen to what they were saying. Leaning out the window to hear, Megan managed to catch Gus saying to Uncle Frank, "Well, I'm with you. It had to be a dream. I don't see how it could be real."

With that, Grandma's plans were literally out the window. Megan jumped out of the car first and then me. The dream argument started all over again. Grandma, this time, only let it go on for a few short moments. She knew this had to end because it was now really getting late.

"Listen, everyone," she said with an uncharacteristic firmness that definitely got our attention. Grandpa smiled to himself from inside the car. I figured that he probably had seen that side of her before. "You're never going to solve this argument, and it's time to go. Let's just leave it that we all agree that the cloud people are real, and that's that. As for the rest, we'll discuss that next year. Now Megan and Billy, get in the car. And you too, Uncle Frank!"

There was no question now that the evening was over! We said our goodbyes to Gus and jumped in the car. As we pulled away, Grandpa, leaned out the window and said goodbye for all of us.

"So long for now!"

Gus smiled and waved back. I think he knew. I think we all knew that we would see each other again. I'm sure that he couldn't wait, any more than we could. I could almost read his mind. It was as if I could hear him saying to himself, *I knew I wasn't crazy. I'm so glad I met them, and I can't wait till next summer.*

Then it struck me. Was I becoming like the cloud people? How could I know what he was thinking?

I don't know if we were all talked out, but it was a quiet ride home. I guess each of us was caught up in our own thoughts. It really had been an amazing couple of days!

The Last Day

That night I didn't go flying, I didn't dream, and I also didn't do much sleeping. I just lay there thinking back over the last few days. I smiled as I remembered that first night when I met the cloud people. I even laughed a little as I thought about all of our debates and discussions. I think my favorite was the night that Megan and I were flying and that great game of sevens. The images of all that I had done over these few days were racing through my mind. Then I got really sad. I felt like crying but no tears came. I couldn't believe that I had to leave in the morning. I wanted so badly to stay. I knew this was just the beginning. I almost burst from all the emotions running through me. I tried to remember Grandpa's advice, but it just wasn't helping. I thought of Megan's encouragement, but even that didn't make my sadness go away. I couldn't stand it. What was I going to do?

As I lay there thinking and thinking and thinking, still wide awake, I began to wonder what everyone else was doing. What were they thinking? Everything was quiet, but I thought I heard voices. I think Grandpa and Grandma were talking. I was tempted to go to their room to see if they were awake. I just wanted to talk with them but decided to leave them alone. It was the middle of the night, and I couldn't bring myself to bother them. Then I wondered what Megan was doing. I know these days were also special to her. What was she thinking? We had always been good friends, but now I realized how much she meant to me. All that happened was great, but it was even greater because she was a part of it. I didn't know how I was going to say goodbye in the morning. And, what about Uncle Frank? He always had that tough exterior and was always ready to question and challenge, but I wondered, deep down, what did he really think? He tried to make us believe that he was a sarcastic skeptic, but I think he really was a softie. I think he really believed me and Megan but just wanted to bust our chops. I eventually drifted off to sleep, but I definitely didn't get much that night. Normally, I could doze a little on the plane, but I knew that on the return trip, I would be looking out the window for clouds. No, there wouldn't be any catch-up sleep on the plane.

Finally, I woke up from one of my short naps and wondered what time it was. Just when I went to look at the clock, my alarm went off. I couldn't believe that it was morning. I was tired and wished I had been able to get some sleep, but even more, I wished I didn't have to go. I knew that I had no choice. I had to get up and pack. As I got out of bed and my feet hit the floor, I stopped for a moment, and to psyche myself up for having to leave, I walked over to the mirror, looked at myself, and pointed my finger. "Look here, Billy. Remember. This isn't over. There's more to come!" With that little pep talk, I began my preparations for leaving.

Breakfast was quiet. Everyone was a little sad. I don't think anybody knew what to say, and I had a hard time even looking at anyone. In fact, everyone had their heads down as we continued to eat our breakfast in silence. I don't how I managed to do it, but remembering that Mom would ask me if I thanked Grandpa and Grandma, I picked my head up and looked at them and said. "Well, thanks, Grandpa and Grandma, for a great vacation. Thanks for everything."

They just nodded but didn't say anything. We all just continued to eat without talking. I should have known, but it was Uncle Frank who finally broke the spell of sadness that was hanging over the breakfast table. "Hey, Billy and Megan, between now and next summer, I'm going to work on this flying business. I'll bet by then, I'll be so good that I'll be faster than either of you!"

That's all he had to say. I took the bait, and Megan was right behind. Breakfast came alive. We were laughing and jabbing at each other again. Grandpa and Grandma smiled at each other. I think they were happy that Uncle Frank had broken the mood. I was too because I don't think I would have been able to leave if we just continued to sit in silence. Those last minutes of laughter brought back the joy of my time there. It was the boost I needed.

It was Grandpa who finally made the announcement that it was time to leave. "Sorry to break up this party, but it's time to go. I'm going to miss you, Billy. I know that you don't want to leave, but like I once told you, that's part of life. We have to be grateful for what we have. Besides, it can be nice to leave wanting a little more. It's good to have something to look forward to—like next summer! So what do you say? Let's get this show on the road, and we'll see you next year!"

Indeed, it was time. I walked upstairs for the last time on that trip and got my suitcase and backpack. Even though I wanted to delay as much as possible, I could hear Mom and Dad telling me to get ready. I also wanted to respect my grandparents. I couldn't keep them waiting. So ready or not, my suitcase was packed, and I was coming back down the stairs. As I reached the first floor, I realized that everyone was already outside. When I walked out the door onto the porch, they were standing by the car. The trunk was open, waiting for my suitcase. I walked over, put it in, and Uncle Frank closed the trunk.

I went over to Grandpa and Grandma and gave them both a big hug. "Thanks for everything. You two are the best! This was so great. Thanks."

I gave each of them one more hug. Megan was standing near them with a little tear on her cheek. We had become even better friends over these last few days, and our new adventure with the cloud people made it even more special.

"I wish you lived closer," she managed to say.

I did too. It was hard to say goodbye. I gave her a big hug. As I stepped back, maybe using a little bit of Uncle Frank's strategy, I told her, "Who knows, even though we'll be apart, maybe we'll go flying some night! As fast as you are, you could be at my house in no time! Anything is possible!"

She smiled at me and added, "You never know!"

As if we planned it, we then turned to Uncle Frank. "Maybe you could join us."

I couldn't believe that he didn't have a comeback. He smiled, but I think he too was sad. After a brief pause, he finally said, "Well, Billy. It's time. I sure am going to miss you." The long pause that followed really convinced me that he did have a soft side. Then he continued, "We don't want you to be late for your plane. As Grandpa said, 'Let's get this show on the road.'"

Before I got in the car, I had to take one last look around. Then I looked up at the sky. I was looking for clouds, but all of a sudden, I saw something that almost took my breath away. There was something hanging from a branch on the tree by the house. I froze in my tracks and stared. I was pointing to it, but no one else saw it. I think they thought I was pointing to a cloud, but the sky was clear.

I started mumbling, "Can it be? Can it be?"

"What's up, Billy?" Uncle Frank asked.

"What are you looking at?" Megan asked. "I don't see any clouds."

"No. Not the clouds. The tree. Look at the tree. What's that dangling from that branch?" Disappointed that's all I meant, Megan said, "Who knows? Probably just a piece of paper."

"No, it's not a piece of paper?" I then began frantically searching the ground for a stick or something to throw. I'm sure they were all thinking that I had just lost my mind, but I had to find a stick. At last I found one and, without explanation, gave it a toss at the branch.

I missed, and Grandpa excitedly said, "Be careful. Don't break a window."

I was so focused on my mission that I barely heard him. I ran and retrieved the stick and gave it another toss, again with no luck. Everyone was starting to laugh a little and Grandma said, "Okay, Billy. That's enough. We have to go."

I think that's the first time I ever disrespected Grandma, but I was obsessed. If that was what I thought it was in the tree, I had to knock it down. I made one more attempt, this time managing to hit my prize, but it remained stuck on the tree.

Realizing that I wasn't going to quit, Uncle Frank intervened. "Look, we have to get going. Let me have a try."

He grabbed the stick and gave it a toss. It was a direct hit, and my mystery object came floating down. I ran over and picked it up. I started jumping up and down and showing it to them as if it was an award that I had been given.

"I knew it! I knew it!"

"Knew what?" asked Megan.

Without answering her, I turned, "Uncle Frank, hurry. Open the trunk. I need my suitcase."

"Why?" he asked.

"Please. I'll explain. I have to check something."

He just shrugged his shoulders and popped open the trunk. I ran over and got my suitcase. I opened it up and rummaged through my packed clothes till I found what I was looking for. Fortunately, they didn't try to stop my frantic searching. They just stood by the trunk, wondering what I was doing. At last, I grabbed what I needed, my pajamas, the ones that I had been using the whole time. Without explaining, I picked them up to show them.

"Look at this," I said. "They're ripped. Remember?" I then grabbed my mysterious prize and slowly placed it in the spot where the pajama pants were ripped. It was a perfect fit. It was like putting the final piece in a puzzle. "Look. This is the missing piece. It wasn't ripped when I came. Remember when we noticed it was torn, but we didn't know how?"

At first everyone just stood there as if they were looking at a crazy person. Suddenly, Megan blurted out, "Wow. That's it. The night you flew. That's how the pants were ripped. When you went out the window, they must have gotten caught on the branch. How else could that piece be up there. It's true. It's true. There's your proof!"

Everyone stood with their mouths open, most of all, Uncle Frank. He just stared at the evidence presented to him. I stood there with a huge grin on my face as I continued to hold up the pajama pants and the torn piece that indeed fit perfectly.

Grandma looked at Grandpa as if to say, "Can it be?"

Uncle Frank finally spoke. As he stared at my pajamas, he spoke in a slow, deliberate voice, "It can't be. It just can't be."

"What other explanation could there be?" Megan asked. "We didn't go climbing in our pajamas. We weren't up that far in the tree. How else could it get there? There's your proof. It's right in front of you. It was real. It couldn't have been a dream!"

Up until that moment, I was filled with sadness at leaving. Now I was filled with excitement. This was the best vacation ever. I looked at everyone as I continued to hold up my evidence.

"Now I really can't wait until next summer! And next year, I'm bringing my camera!"

About the Author

The author has been a Catholic priest for forty-two years, currently serving as pastor of a large parish in Southern New Jersey. He had a wonderful childhood growing up in a small town in New Jersey with his three brothers and one sister and feels blessed to have been raised by parents who were part of the greatest generation. His father was a World War II veteran who decided to write down his experiences before he died. His mother was the glue of the family but died of breast cancer before he was ordained.

The family took many great vacations and camping trips, and it was during those trips that his imagination grew. Between the experiences shared and time talking around the campfire, his love of storytelling grew. Once he became a pastor, writing was an important part of his ministry and communication with the flock. It has been his custom each year to write a short story or reflection as his Christmas gift to families and friends.

The purpose of his writings was always to share faith and to encourage people in their lives.

It was during a trip to visit his brother in Tennessee that the idea for his book was born as he looked out the window at the clouds. Instead of a short story, this idea became a book. The purpose was to encourage children to use their imaginations and also reinforce traditional morals and encourage the development of good character.

He has been a happy and dedicated priest, and he seeks to reflect his love of life and a positive attitude in all he does.

CPSIA information can be obtained
at www.ICGtesting.com
Printed in the USA
LVHW040453040423
743404LV00001B/33